THEIR STATUS - RIVALRY

Author

Mauj

Copyright © 2025 Mauj

Disclaimer

The following disclaimer applies to "Title of the Book, 'THEIR STATUS-RIVALRY', authored by, Mauj:

1. **Fictional Nature**: This is a work of fiction intended for entertainment purposes only. Any similarities to actual events, persons, or organizations, whether real or fictional, are purely coincidental. The characters, teams, and events depicted in this story are fictional and designed to enhance the narrative. Scenarios may include exaggerated or unrealistic portrayals of sports events, athlete behaviors, and outcomes. This story does not reflect the realities of professional sports and should not be interpreted as an accurate representation of any athletes or competitions. The author and publisher assume no responsibility for any interpretations, actions, or consequences resulting from engaging with this story.

2. **Legal Advice**: The legal scenarios presented in this book are fictional and crafted for dramatic effect. They do not necessarily reflect real-life courtroom practices or legal systems. While efforts have been made to ensure accuracy in the depiction of legal principles, laws vary by jurisdiction and are subject to change. Readers should consult a qualified legal professional for specific legal advice. The representation of legal professionals and courtroom procedures in this book should not be construed as actual legal advice or accurate portrayals of real court experiences. The author and publisher disclaim any liability arising from the use or misuse of the information contained within this book.

3. **Medical Disclaimer**: Any medical facts, references to health, and mental health-related information in this book are purely fictional and intended for entertainment purposes only. These depictions are created solely to advance the narrative and add dramatic elements. The author makes no claims regarding their accuracy and encourages readers to seek professional medical advice for any health-related concerns.

4. **Copyright**: This book is protected under copyright law. All rights are reserved. No part of this book may be reproduced, distributed, or transmitted in any form or by any means, including photocopying, recording, or other electronic or mechanical methods, without prior written permission from the author or publisher, except where permitted by law.

5. **Liability Limitation**: The author and publisher shall not be liable for any damages arising from the use or inability to use this book, including but not limited to direct, indirect, incidental, or consequential damages. This includes damages resulting from errors, omissions, or inaccuracies in the content.

6. **Public Figures and Situations**: Any references to public figures, companies, or institutions are included for context and narrative enhancement. Such references do not imply endorsement or association with these entities.

7. **Moral and Ethical Considerations**: The actions and events depicted in this book may not reflect universal moral or ethical standards. Readers are encouraged to engage with the content critically and consider the implications of the narratives presented.

8. **Jurisdiction**: This disclaimer is governed by the laws of [Maharashtra/India], notwithstanding any principles of conflicts of law. Any disputes arising from this book shall be settled in the courts located within [Maharashtra/India]. By reading this book, you acknowledge that you have read, understood, and agree to be bound by this disclaimer.

9. **Theology or Philosophy**: This book is a work of fiction and should not be considered a theological or philosophical guide. The views expressed are those of the characters and may not represent the author's beliefs. Any references to God, atheism, or religion are presented through storytelling and intended as creative literature. Readers are encouraged to critically engage with the material as a dramatization of ideas, not as definitive sources of thought. The author

and publisher do not intend to offend any belief system. For legal, religious, or philosophical guidance, please consult a qualified professional.

10. **Science Fiction**: The technologies, species, and scenarios in this book are products of the author's imagination and should not be interpreted as predictions or endorsements of future developments. The author and publisher do not provide scientific or technical advice and encourage readers to verify any scientific references independently. This speculative work explores theoretical possibilities rather than factual science and should be approached with an open mind and critical perspective.

11. **AI-Generated Images Disclaimer**: Where applicable, this book may include AI-generated images created for illustrative purposes. These images are fictional representations and should not be considered as accurate depictions of real people, places, or events. The author and publisher assume no responsibility for any interpretations or misinterpretations of such images. Any resemblance to real persons, living or dead, is purely coincidental.

Thank you for respecting the creative efforts put into this work.

PROLOGUE

'Rivalry fuels ambition, pushing individuals to be their best.'

Rivalry is a peculiar thing. It is not born out of hatred nor does it necessarily thrive on malice. It is not friendship yet it is not enmity either. It is a strange relationship between two individuals whose paths cross, not because they wish to walk together but because destiny has placed them on the same road, pushing them to measure themselves against each other.

Friendship, they say is about trust, about understanding, about standing side by side, lifting each other up. Rivalry, however is about something else entirely. It is the unspoken challenge between two people who recognize something in the other—a strength, a skill, a fire—that forces them to push beyond their own limits. A rival is not necessarily someone to be destroyed nor a friend to be cherished. A rival is someone who stands as a mirror, reflecting both one's strengths and one's weaknesses, daring them to improve, to grow, to fight—not against the other but against their own limitations.

What does it mean to win? And what does it mean to lose? Victory is often seen as the ultimate validation, the proof that one has surpassed the other. But is that truly what defines success? Perhaps the real battle is not against an opponent but against oneself—the inner fears, the doubts, the voices that whisper of inadequacy. To give one's best, to push beyond the perceived limits, to embrace the struggle with an open heart—this is a victory that no trophy or title can match. And perhaps in that sense, loss is not truly loss but simply another step forward, another lesson learned, another reason to rise and try again.

Between rivals there exists an unspoken understanding. The desire to win is real but so is the respect. They are bound not by affection but by a force just as strong—a relentless drive to test themselves against the best. Theirs is a connection forged in fire, in competition, in an unyielding pursuit of excellence.

Like friendship, rivalry can also be a bond—a bond between two strong and different individuals who are not always bloodthirsty for each other's downfall but are so deeply engaged in their struggle that they become a part of each other's journey. They do not seek destruction; they seek to be better. And through this strange almost paradoxical connection, they push each other toward something greater than either could have achieved alone.

'Rivals are not enemies but forces that challenge and inspire each other.'

CHAPTER 1

ALTITUDE AND ATTITUDE

Nestled in the heart of the ethereal state of Uttarakhand, the snow-capped mountains gleamed like a crown of white diamonds against the serene landscape. Amidst this bewitching beauty, an adventure was set to unfold.

A rugged pickup truck halted at the edge of a snowy mountain road. The iconic jagged peaks pierced the clear blue sky, their pristine allure shining under the high-altitude sun. The SUV door swung open, revealing 'Abeer', a sturdy figure in his twenties. With a grin, he stepped onto the snowy ground.

The boot of the SUV was packed tightly with skiing gear and other related equipment. Keenly, Abeer began unloading the gear, his movements skilled and unhurried. Soon he stood tall at the top of a breathtaking slope, adjusted his skis, tightened his ski boots and gripped his skis firmly as if hoding a sword by its hilt. With a confidence that belied his one-legged stance, Abeer began his descent. His skiing despite having one amputated leg was nothing short of mesmerizing, a jaw-dropping display of skill that instantly captivated anyone who witnessed it.

Consequently, another car came to a halt at the base of the slope. 'Neet', in a flurry of motion rushed out. Meanwhile, Abeer gracefully concluded his stunning skiing descent and reached the bottom of the slope. Neet ran up to him, her breath coming fast in the cold air.

"What kind of madness is this, Abeer? You'll make us miss the flight today!" she exclaimed, a combination of worry and urgency in her voice.

Abeer, smiling warmly responded, *"Well, I can't pack these mountains and take them to Delhi, so I was just making the most of my three-day stint before my skiing hiatus."*

Exasperated, Neet handed Abeer his walking stick and headed back towards her car, leaving Abeer smiling as he watched her retreat.

A plane touched down smoothly on the runway at Delhi airport, signaling the start of a new chapter in Abeer's arduous and challenging life. Inside the grand corridors of a lavish five-star hotel Abeer with Neet by his side, entered a packed conference hall. The room burst into applause, standing as a testament to Abeer's inspiring journey. Banners bearing the title 'Fitrat (Human nature/Temperament)' adorned the walls indicating the grand launch of Abeer's book. As they settled at the podium for a Q&A session, a reporter questioned the book's title suggesting that it should better reflect the story's theme with a name like "Snow Leopard, Avalanche" or "Icy Storm," expressing bewilderment over the unusual Persian name "Fitrat"

Abeer, with a knowing smile explained, *"I think you missed the core essence of the story. This book talks about my greatest rival. If you have a strong contender, you don't need a girlfriend. He will keep you awake at night more than anyone else."* Laughter rippled through the hall. He added, *"Such was the nature of Rohil. Since the story delves into the volatile dynamics of two fierce opponents, the title "Fitrat" was deemed fitting."*

Another reporter requested Abeer to read a few lines from his favorite chapter of the book. Holding the book up for everyone to see Abeer stated, *"The entire book is my favorite,"* he flips open the book and dives right into the story from the page it landed on.

As he began to read the lights in the hall dimmed, focusing a spotlight solely on him. With the muffled sounds of a commentator beginning to fade in, Abeer narrated,

"It was the first day of the 'Frozen Himalayan competition'. The temperature plunged to a chilly -5 degrees, and I was sweating."

The merging worlds of the book and the present created a spellbinding narration, leaving the audience captivated by the tale of grit, determination and the boundless beauty of the Himalayas.

The icy chill on the morning of 'The Frozen Himalayan competition' 2023, was so intense that every breath felt like inhaling shards of ice, turning the day into a dramatic dance of frost and snow. One of the most sought-after and toughest competitions in the adventure sports world was about to begin at the grand venue in the Himalayas. The atmosphere was charged, contenders were nervous, and the adrenaline was at its peak. In the biting cold, the commentator announced the start of the tournament. The first event was the ski jump, and the commentator introduced the initial player,

"Welcome, everyone to the electrifying ski jump competition,

where the world's best athletes will defy gravity and race through the sky. Brace yourselves for heart-stopping leaps and spectacular landings as we kick off this incredible event! Our first player of the season is Bruno Botta from Switzerland."

Bruno came to the start point, sat on the bar and awaited the green signal, ready to burst into action. As soon as the green signal appeared Bruno initiated his slide just as he had done the previous year. With perfect balance and impeccable speed, Bruno advanced gracefully. On reaching the take-off point, Bruno executed a magnificent jump landing 2.7 meters ahead of the K-line, thus breaking his own world record. The commentator exclaimed with excitement,

"Wow! Bruno delivers a breathtaking jump and breaks his own record spectacularly!"

Bruno was ecstatic, and his team erupted in celebration, their cheers echoing through the snowy mountains.

Next in line was Abeer Singh, in his early 20s, performing final checks in the holding area. He looked focused, warming up and inspecting his skis.

The commentator introduced Abeer, *"Ready yourselves, folks! Our next competitor is 'Abeer Singh' from India, marking his debut in this competition. Let's cheer him on and wish him the best of luck!"*

Abeer walked towards the starting point with growing tension. Sitting on the bar, Abeer observed young and beautiful, Neet, who approached him from behind and handed him his headgear. Neet highlighted that the forces of nature were in their favour and the wind was blowing perfectly along the direction of the jumping slope. She further emphasized that with this natural advantage, Abeer simply needed to maintain correct posture to achieve the best possible result.

Nervous, Abeer closed his eyes recalling a memory with his father, 'Veer Singh'. Who once told him, Number 1 and number 2 positions are just numbers. A true sportsperson plays to enjoy and experience the game. With this thought in mind, Abeer opened his eyes and began sliding down the slope with firm determination.

The commentator noted as he saw Abeer's impressive speed and posture,

"If he maintains this form for the jump, he could become the first Indian player to capture the fans' attention in this competition."

Abeer reached the take-off point and jumped.

"As expected, his posture is exemplary," the commentator remarked, *"Now let's see where Abeer lands."*

Abeer touched down and the commentator announced excitedly,

"Incredible! Abeer has landed astonishing 3 meters ahead of the K-line, shattering Bruno's record. For the first time in the history of 'The Frozen Himalayan Competition' an Indian player has set a new benchmark! What a historic moment!"

Overjoyed, Neet ran to hug Abeer as spectators applauded his remarkable achievement.

Back in the grand conference hall of the five-star hotel, Abeer finishes reading the excerpt and gently closes the book. He takes a moment to savor the quiet that follows. The lights gradually brighten, casting a soft warm glow over the elegantly decorated room. Abeer takes a deep breath feeling the subtle shift in the air as anticipation builds among the audience. Looking up, he lets a warm genuine smile spread across his face.

"So, that was a glimpse of Fitrat," he announces, his voice carrying a note of satisfaction and pride. The words seem to hang in the air for a moment before the room comes alive with the sound of applause. The audience responds with enthusiastic claps their appreciation filling the space with a vibrant energy. While the applause continues, Abeer reflects on the journey that led him to this moment.

MOUNTAINS OF MEMORIES

The shimmer of a mirage danced on the road, complementing the glint of Abeer's reflection in the car's rear-view mirror. As he journeyed back to his hometown in the Uttarakhand, the winding mountain paths of his memories began to unravel. Images of a young Abeer, around 8 years old, walking through stunning mountain ranges with his father Veer Singh, floated into his mind. Together, they traversed valleys, crossed rivers and rested to drink cool refreshing mountain water. In his recollection, they climbed a steep mountain each step bringing a blend of competition and camaraderie.

Sitting atop a mountain with a bonfire crackling in the backdrop, the past came alive. Filled with spirited determination young Abeer gulped down his milk and triumphantly turned his cup upside down.

"First!" he declared to Veer, "My milk won against your tea."

Veer's laughter rang out warm and hearty. *"At least in this competitive spirit of winning in everything, your mom has instilled the habit of drinking milk in you,"* he said with appreciation.

Abeer, heavily influenced by his mother's go-getter attitude mimicked her advice,

"Only the first position matters; everything that follows is just losing. No matter the endeavor, I always have to win."

Veer's expression turned serious as he placed a comforting hand on Abeer's shoulder. *"You didn't drink your milk, you just finished it,"* he said softly. Abeer looked puzzled. *"In the race to come first, you missed tasting the milk, Abeer,"* Veer explained, handing over a sugar sachet. *"Your milk was bland."*

Feeling chided and unable to comprehend the divergent viewpoints of his parents, Abeer retorted, *"Mom named you Sheikh-Chilli (daydreamer) rightly because your dreams lack the appropriate actions required to achieve them."* Veer only smiled choosing to ignore his son's sarcastic comment, he was fully aware and at peace with his own path in life. Both, carrying their backpacks began to walk towards the horizon.

After their invigorating morning hiking ritual, the morning sun at Abeer's home filtered through the windows, illuminating the dining room where Abeer sat in his school uniform with his father Veer seated beside him.

Veer, an endless chest of wisdom often gently guides his son Abeer through the subtler nuances of life's journey. His insights paint the world with colors of contemplation and understanding. On the other hand, Sunita, Abeer's mother is a self-made industrious professional who views life through the pragmatic lens of practicality and achievements. Her counsel is direct urging Abeer to set clear goals, reach for the stars and strive to attain the best that life has to offer. This dynamic interplay of wisdom versus ambition, reflection versus practicality often leaves Abeer oscillating between two worlds, trying to harmonize his father's philosophical musings with his mother's goal-oriented ethos.

The scent of breakfast filled the air as Abeer's mother Sunita balanced preparing breakfast while working on her iPad. Veer, immersed in a sea of contemplation continued imparting his wisdom to Abeer. Picking up the threads of their conversation from that morning's invigorating hike,

"Hard work is something which many people can do but talent is rare. A true sportsman gives their 100% with both talent and effort, leaving the outcome to destiny."
Sunita, emerging from the kitchen while talking on her mobile phone overheard their conversation. She quickly ended the call, set her iPad on the table, took off her apron and placed it on a chair. Sunita chose her

words with precision during their intense debate and pointed out a flaw in Veer's statement. She firmly told Abeer,

"Destiny isn't handed to you on a silver platter; it's something you craft with your own hands. Make yourself so invincible that even destiny has no choice but to bow down and clear a path for you. In this world, it's not about how much talent you possess or how hard you strive—people only care about the results you deliver." Her declaration was a potent blend of realism and ambition, reflecting her unwavering belief in the power of determined effort.

This stark contrast in his parents' philosophies was a frequent topic of debate at home, yet Abeer often navigated these waters with humor and intelligence. He glanced at the wall clock and mockingly said to Veer, *"Papa, it's volcano eruption time."* Abeer then whispered urgently, *"Or should I rather say, Mom's office departure time. Remember our pact: never argue with Mom when she's hungry and when she's about to leave for work. Follow these rules and there will be peace at home. Just stay quiet and don't respond."* His words carried the playful yet strategic wisdom of a son well-versed with the family's morning routine. Both Abeer and Veer giggled their lighthearted bond shining through even in moments of tension.

Sunita soon returned hurriedly to pick up her apron and noticing father-son's amusement, she advised Abeer,

"Leave your father's company," She demanded, giving Veer a piercing look, *"His views about life are gravely misguided and won't lead you anywhere,"* she warned. Her eyes filled with conviction and the protective instincts of a mother. Despite her stern words Abeer's respect and admiration for his mother was evident.

With a confidence towering higher than the tallest Himalayan peaks, Abeer pointed to himself and declared,

"Mom, could you please spare me from this bickering?" In fact, you should show some respect to the future champion of the Frozen Himalayan competition. Just wait and see—you'll have to stand in line for my autograph!"
Sunita became visibly furious after noticing Abeer mimicking Veer's

ideology. She turned to Veer and reprimanded him,

"Please, stop ruining his life too. At least give him some sensible career options," Sunita insisted, frustration evident in her voice. *"As if handling one sportsperson at home wasn't enough, now you're trying to shape Abeer into another version of yourself."*

Veer immediately sprang to his own defense, *"I've never pushed Abeer toward competition. If climbing is in his DNA, what can I do about it?"* A helpless expression clouding his face.

"Shut up, Veer," Sunita retorted, her exasperation evident.

Turning her attention back to Abeer, who was about to speak, Sunita interrupted with a stern look and instructed both to keep an ear out for the pressure-cooker in the kitchen. *"Turn it off after three whistles, or we'll be having burnt chicken for lunch."* This was Sunita's signature method of restoring order in the household whenever arguments like these erupted.

As Sunita left the room the first whistle of the pressure cooker blew. Seizing the opportunity, Veer reacted to Sunita's comment with lighthearted sarcasm, saying, *"Thank goodness for the cooker's whistle. It just saved us from the hot lava of your mother's temper."*

Abeer, whose camaraderie with his father was more like that of close friends, grinned and suggested, *"Papa, you should win the Frozen Himalayan competition and prove to Mom that you really are my father. Once you set foot on something, you won't relent until you come out with flying colors."*

Veer, amused by his son's advice, replied with a chuckle, *"I don't think Sunita doubts that I'm your father. She always questions my potential to achieve anything worthwhile in life."* Just then, the second whistle of the pressure cooker blew, punctuating the moment.
Turning serious, Veer confided in Abeer, *"I don't have what it takes to be a winner. Climbing is the only thing I know and I'm confident enough to do it with the best of my abilities. But winning a competition requires a different skill set—one that I lack. Management professionals like your mother excel at that."*

Understanding his father's struggle and wanting to strengthen their bond, Abeer tried to lift his spirits. *"Chill, Papa, chill,"* he said with a grin. Just then the third whistle blew and both got up from the table to turn off the gas stove.

Veer paused for a moment, then smiled at Abeer and said, *"Today your mom's temper is pretty high. Let's help her cool down."* Sparking excitement in Abeer, who eagerly anticipated the plan brewing in his father's mind.

Sunita, almost ready to dash off to the office, steps into the living room and stops in her tracks as she noticed a beautifully arranged breakfast on the table. She approaches the dining table to have a closer look, immediately Veer with a soft smile and elegant motion pulls out a chair with a flourish.

"Please, Mom, have a seat," Abeer says, guiding her gently. Once she is seated, Veer deftly pushes the chair back into place and with a coordinated grace Abeer places a napkin on her lap, while Veer lifts the cover off the juice glass. This synchronized effort leaves Sunita momentarily astonished. She takes a tentative bite of her breakfast and with a twinkle of sarcasm in her eye remarks,

"Anyone can make breakfast on a whim for one day. The real talent lies in making breakfast every day and still making it to the office on time."

Veer and Abeer, hands folded courteously chime in together,

"Dear Sunita ji, as a father and son duo, we would like to extend our heartfelt thanks for everything you do for us and beyond." Abeer, ever the charmer, takes it a step further in showing appreciation. With a mischievous gleam in his eye he warmly says, *"Please accept our deepest gratitude and enjoy the most delicious breakfast, lovingly prepared by Chef Veer under the expert guidance of Senior Chef Abeer."* They exchange a conspiratorial wink and continue in unison, *"With a sweet kiss."*

Leaning in they each plant a tender peck on Sunita's cheek before Abeer grabs his bag. With exaggerated speed both he and Veer dart out of the house. Leaving Sunita to call after them with a playful smirk,

"This won't achieve anything, chef Abeer. If you truly want to impress me, come first in your class."

The bonfire warmth on that mountain top was akin to the warmth of Abeer's family bond. It was a space where love, competition and understanding coexisted. The subtle humor, the deep respect for his mother and the playful yet wise interactions with his father added depth to his treasured memories, teaching him to navigate life's dynamics gracefully.

Veer and his son Abeer strolled along the bustling city sidewalk heading towards Abeer's school. The morning sun cast long shadows as they walked side by side.

"Do you think you'll come first in class again this time?" Veer asked, his tone both curious and challenging.

"100%, Papa," Abeer replied with a confident grin. *"Have I ever come second before?"*

Veer raised his finger and made a writing gesture in the air. *"When you write the number one, it's just a simple straight line. But remember, overconfidence can make you slide down from the top in an instant. If you fall backwards, you become zero. Fall forward, and you crash into number two."*

"Wrong, Papa," Abeer countered, his eyes sparkling with determination. *"You can maintain the number one spot too."*

"Only with humility, by being humble," Veer said, pausing for effect. *"Actually, I find the number two position more interesting."*

Abeer laughed mockingly, *"Don't say that in front of Mom, or she'll have a field day with you."*

Veer smirked and made another writing gesture in the air. *"But I'm serious. Look at the construction of number '2'—a semicircle on top, a slanting line through the middle, a bend at the bottom, followed by a straight line. It's more complex."*

Veer fell silent, his gaze fixed on the distant peaks. The wind rustled through the trees, carrying the weight of unspoken words. It was as if he was gathering his thoughts, preparing to say something that would etch itself into Abeer's soul—something that would stay with him long after this moment had passed, shaping the course of his life in ways he could not yet understand.

"The number two position is a blessing in disguise," Veer said, gazing at the horizon. *"It keeps you grounded, keeps your hunger alive. Being number one, on the other hand, is a dangerous place to be. It feeds your ego, makes you believe you're invincible. But the moment you taste ultimate success, fear grips you. You start to wonder—how long before someone takes my place? And once that fear sets in, it's only a matter of time before you fall."*

Abeer frowned, kicking a small rock down the road. He had always been taught to aim for the top, to be the best. But his father's words painted a different picture.

"But isn't it frustrating?" Abeer asked, his voice laced with the weight of his own struggles as a student. *"What about the people who try their hardest but still can't reach number one? What happens to them?"*

Veer chuckled, placing a firm yet gentle hand on Abeer's shoulder. His touch was warm, reassuring like the steady presence of the mountains themselves.

"That's not frustration, son," he said. *That's desire* and *desire isn't necessarily your enemy—it just needs to be understood. The truth is, not everyone is meant to be at the top. And those who do make it often find themselves lonelier than they expected. Life isn't about claiming the highest peak. It's about understanding which path truly makes you happy."*

Abeer listened, though his young mind wrestled with the idea.

"If you view life from a wider perspective," Veer continued, *"you'll see that everything—winning and losing, success and failure, even right and wrong—is in constant flux, striving for equilibrium. And that equilibrium is happiness. The place you are in right now, at this very moment, is exactly where you are meant to be. And if you accept that, no sorrow, no frustration, no unfulfilled desire will ever shake you. You will be at peace."*

Abeer let the words sink in as the wind whispered through the valley. Somewhere deep inside, a quiet understanding began to take root. Perhaps happiness wasn't about conquering the highest peak but about discovering a rhythm—a quiet harmony woven into the journey itself.

As they reached the gate of the school, Veer held onto Abeer's hand for a moment longer. *"By the way your teacher emailed me your result last evening. You stood second in the class this time."* Veer informed Abeer with a smirk.

Abeer stopped in his tracks, stunned by the news. His school bag slipped from his hand, landing with a thud on the ground.

FORMIDABLE CAREER CHOICES

Nurtured by a unique blend of introspection and drive, Abeer emerged as a gifted polymath. His academic excellence and fervent love for climbing defined his college days, cultivating a competitive spirit rooted deeply in integrity, sincerity, and unwavering honesty.

The 10th Inter-college annual wall climbing Competition buzzed with excitement, drawing participants from colleges far and wide. As the venue pulsed with energy, the MC's voice resonated through the speakers,

"Abeer and Neet from 'Sindhu College', please come forward and take your positions at the start point." Amidst final checks, Abeer and Neet raised their hands, prompting a wave of enthusiastic cheers from their supporters.

The MC then called out for Rohil and Pia. The crowd scanned the area searching for Rohil and Pia but they were nowhere to be seen despite repeated announcements. Undeterred, the MC continued,

"Perhaps Rohil and Pia are strategizing their game plan. Meanwhile, let's move on to our next contenders."

As the contenders gathered at the base of the climbing wall, a palpable sense of anticipation filled the air. The lineup, bristling with determination and camaraderie reflected the intensity of the moment. The collective energy of the venue surged, echoing the thrill of what was to come. Both participants and their supporters brimming with excitement, ready to embark on the gripping challenge that awaited them. It was the kind of scene where dreams were poised to ascend to new heights. ---

On a crisp morning in a polished suburban neighborhood, Rohil, a young and energetic guy in his early 20's claded in a tracksuit was in a rush. Eager to make up for lost time he swiftly grabbed his backpack and mounted his sports bicycle. As he pedaled energetically through the sleek streets, his progress came to an abrupt halt due to a massive traffic jam clogging the main road.

Refusing to be defeated by gridlock, Rohil veered onto a secluded shortcut that wound its way through wilderness. Here, the true extent of his cycling prowess came to life. Navigating through a maze of natural obstacles, he effortlessly performed acrobatic feats with his bike. He surged over rocks and shallow river, crossed precarious broken bridge and even rode along narrow train tracks.

Rohil's daring adventure continued as he leaped over rustic haystack and descended steep flights of steps with incredible dexterity. Each dangerous stunt he executed was a testament to his mastery of cycling, blending skill and fearless determination. In the heart of the outback with each twist and turn Rohil demonstrated that he was no ordinary sportsperson; he was a master of his craft. Unafraid to take on the wildest of challenges.

Finally, Rohil arrived at the energetic wall climbing venue, skidding his bike to a halt right in front of Pia, who stood with her arms crossed and eyes blazing with anger. Without missing a beat, she declared with fierce determination, *"I'll lead the climb today."*

Rohil, still catching his breath, tried to keep his composure.

"Pia, in all our practice sessions I was always the lead climber. Why didn't you say earlier that you wanted to take the lead? We could have adjusted and practiced with that formation from the start. Changing our roles at the last minute? It's reckless and could lead to disastrous consequences—a misstep, lost balance and we'd both risk a dangerous fall. We can't afford that kind of chaos in the competition."

Without missing a beat, Pia snapped back, fuming, *"You never gave me the chance to lead. Every time I tried to speak up you dismissed and ignored my input, patronising me with that condescending 'baby' moniker. I was just an innocent girl, always falling into your trap and blindly following your lead, believing you knew best. But look where that's gotten us now."*

The simmering tension between them finally erupted into a storm of words, each retort sharper and louder than the last as their tempers flared uncontrollably.

Rohil sighed, attempting to defuse the tension. *"Try to understand, Pia. To lead, you need both agility and strength."*

Pia's eyes narrowed, her voice rising with indignation. *"What do you mean, I'm weak? You clearly have no idea about girl power, Rohil."*

"That's not what I meant," Rohil said, his voice pleading for reason. *"If we show even a bit of carelessness, we'll lose."*

Pia's expression hardened. *"So winning is more important to you than your girlfriend's happiness?"*

"Of course...umm," Rohil stammered, realizing his mistake, but it was too late. Pia's fury ignited afresh. *"I mean, we compete only to win, isn't it?."*

"Even if it means losing your relationship?" Pia cried out. *"I was foolish to take you for granted all this while. Deep down, I knew you were selfish but I held on because I loved you. But today marks the final straw. Now I see clearly—you'd let everything we have fall apart for the sake of this one competition."* Her words cut through the air like daggers, each one striking harder than the last.

Rohil, equally frustrated, responded firmly, *"Pia, you're blowing this out of proportion. Emotions are a double-edged sword; they can either make you or break you. Be wise and use them to your advantage. Right now, we're here to climb not to get entangled in boyfriend-girlfriend drama. Our focus should be on the competition."*

"To hell with your competition and to hell with you!" Pia exploded, her voice trembling with anger. *"First, you show up late and then you act all high and mighty. And guess what? The competition has already started, I was merely testing your small-minded attitude. Forget me, Rohil. From now on our relationship ceases to exist."* She turned on her heel, her declaration echoing as she stormed away.

Rohil took a deep breath, his expression steeling. *"Oh, so all this drama was just to end the relationship?"* he shouted after her. *"If only you had told me earlier! We could've thrown a breakup party and parted like civilized adults. But I guess maturity isn't really your thing. Goodbye, baby."* Without a backward glance, Rohil turned and walked in the opposite direction, his resolve unshaken.

Rohil clutched his steaming coffee cup and maneuvered through the boisterous crowd to find the perfect vantage point to watch the wall climbing competition. As the referee blew the starting whistle, the audience's roar filled the air, a chorus of excitement that seemed almost tangible.

Abeer and Neet shot forward from the very first moment, their ascent confident and swift. Rohil's eyes immediately fixed on their progress. Leaning slightly toward the girl beside him, he asked,

"Who are those two?"

The girl, her eyes glued to the climbers, answered without hesitation, *"They're the pride of Sindhu College. If Abeer and Neet are competing, no one else stands a chance."*
Rohil, ever perceptive, quickly assessed their skill. *"Bro, your friends look pretty pro,"* he remarked. *"Or maybe they're just lucky today because I'm not out there. If I were competing, this title would be mine, no contest."*

The girl turned to him, her expression unimpressed. *"You're quite full of yourself, aren't you? Or should I say arrogant?"*

Rohil chuckled, unbothered by her retort. *"Just replace 'arrogance' with 'confidence,' and you've nailed it. I am full of confidence. By the way, can I get you a cup of coffee?"*

She shook her head, her reply curt. *"No thanks."*

Rohil picked up his bag and began to walk away but the girl's voice stopped him. *"Mr. Big Shot, why don't you stick around and see who actually wins?"*

Without turning, Rohil declared over his shoulder, *"Congratulations in advance. Your friends will win—unless they happen to face someone like me."*

His swagger as he walked away was a testament to his attitude, a man completely sure of himself and his abilities.

The morning sunbathed the lavish Dhoot residence in a golden glow. After the competition Rohil pedaled up the driveway, his backpack slung over one shoulder. As he dismounted his bicycle at the entrance, he found his father Rajinder Dhoot, a man renowned for his journey from rags to riches, preparing to leave for work. Rajinder, perpetually alert and driven, paused as he saw Rohil approaching.

"So have you filled out the distance learning form?" Rajinder asked with a hint of sarcasm, knowing well that his son had yet to comply with his wishes. Behind Rohil, his mother stood, her eyes communicating a reluctant complicity.

Rohil sighed, sensing the impending confrontation but decided to keep the mood light. *"Dad, regular college is a waste of time. Time is money and after all I am the son of the great Rajinder Singh Dhoot."*

Rajinder's expression didn't soften. *"And what do you plan to do with all this time you save?"* He began walking towards his sleek car, forcing Rohil to follow. Determined and a bit excited, Rohil launched into his pitch,

"Dad, I want to create an adventure sports app. It will list all the adventure sports in India, and we'll offer courses and expeditions as well."

His father remained unmoved, clinging to his pragmatic wisdom. *"In my opinion, you should qualify to study 'STEM' will send you to America for higher studies."*

Refusing to be dissuaded, Rohil pressed on. *"Dad, I have the whole project report ready. I can come to the office and give you a presentation."*

But Rajinder's stance was unwavering. *"If you want to get into start-up then you will receive only the basics from me—food, clothes, and shelter. Everything else, you must earn on your own. That's how I did it."*

Rohil clenched his fists, his jaw tightening as his father's words sank in. A storm of frustration swirled within him, but he held it back, forcing a strained smile. His father's unyielding stance felt like a wall he couldn't break through—solid, immovable, and maddeningly indifferent. He had hoped for understanding, maybe even a sliver of compromise, but instead, he was met with the same rigid beliefs, the same dismissive tone. Every counterpoint he made was effortlessly swatted away, leaving him feeling unheard, insignificant.

Rohil watched as his father opened the car door, emotions simmering. *"Then I don't need anything from you. I am a genius; I can do everything by myself. Thank you."* He turned his back defiantly but couldn't resist glancing around the opulent estate. *"I'll buy all this very soon,"* he declared, his voice filled with unspoken anguish.

Rajinder's smile was tinged with a trace of mockery. *"It's the enthusiasm of youth. When you step out of this pampered world, you will face the real challenges."* Their eyes met, locking in a silent clash of profoundly opposing worlds.

With a final, dismissive glance, Rohil's father drove away, leaving a scar on his son's soul—one that would shape him forever, turning disappointment into something far deeper. ---

Concurrently Abeer burst into his home, excitement radiating from him as he handed the gleaming trophy to his mother. Sunita, however, barely glanced at it before setting it aside. She with a sigh, sinks into the couch, looks visible disappointment. *"Abeer,"* she began, her voice gentle but firm, *"what has been the one constant in your life since childhood?"*

With a warm smile, Abeer approached and enveloped her in a hug. *"You, Mom,"* he replied sincerely.

Her face remained serious. *"Then for always being there for you, I believe I'm owed something in return,"* she said, her tone heavy with expectation.

Confused, Abeer stepped back. *"What do you mean?"* he asked.

Sunita rose from the couch and moved towards the desktop, her demeanor resolute. *"Promise me that you will never become a climber,"* she stated flatly.

Abeer was taken aback. *"What? Mom, I love climbing. Things are different now. I want to study mountaineering professionally."*

Ignoring his passion, Sunita opened a drawer and pulled out a form, handing it to him. *"Fill this out and sign it,"* she commanded.

Abeer looked down at the form and his heart sank. *"Mom, you know I've never been good at science, technology, or mathematics. How can I succeed in STEM?"* he protested.

Sunita's eyes bored into his. *"Despite not liking them, you still score the highest marks in math and science. If you grow to appreciate them, you'll have a brilliant career,"* she reasoned.

Exasperated, Abeer said, *"Mom, you very well know parents shouldn't impose their wishes on their children. They should let them choose their own paths in life."*

Her eyes welled up with unshed tears. *"Those are just nice words, Abeer. The mountain took your father from us. I despise this sport,"* she confessed. On her desktop screen the image of his dad, Veer Singh flashed as the screensaver.

Abeer pointed to the screen to console her. *"First, you need to let go of Dad's photo. You can't stay trapped in the past forever."*

Sunita's composure snapped. *"Shut up, Abeer. How dare you speak that way?"* she spat.

Kneeling before her and holding her hands tightly, Abeer tried to soothe her turmoil. *"Mom, we can't change what happened. It's been five years since Dad passed. You can't keep hoping for his return. People don't come back."*

Sunita stood abruptly, still furious. *"Don't try to teach me, Abeer. Understand this: you can only pursue mountaineering over my dead body and I plan on living a very long life "*
She pressed the form into his hands, her eyes brimming with tears.

"I can't lose you too, Abeer." His resolve wavered as he reluctantly accepted the form, feeling the heavy burden of her fears and his unfulfilled dreams.

THE SKI JUMP SAGA

In the narrative of the book 'Fitrat', which elegantly intertwines past and present, the tale oscillates between the high-stakes drama of 'The Frozen Himalayan' competition and the formative years of its protagonists, Abeer and Rohil. Having explored their college days, the story returns to the gripping ski jump event of 'The Frozen Himalayan' competition 2023, where Abeer had already held an impressive lead with his magnificent jump.

Next in line was the contender 'Zak Speed' from the United Kingdom. Last year's runner-up, Zak Speed, stood at the crest of the slope, his figure etched against the bright expanse of the frosty mountains. The air was electric with anticipation as Zak set off. 'Zak Speed' is on the move, racing down the track with the memories of last year's near victory fueling his descent. Zak neared the takeoff point, his muscles coiled like springs before he leapt into the air.

The commentator's voice took on a critical edge, *"Zak Speed has taken flight, though his takeoff wasn't as forceful as we might have hoped. But there's still everything to play for."*

The crowd's collective gaze followed Zak through his arc in the sky, a silent witness to his airborne endeavor.

"Remember, in ski jumping, the landing is where champions are made or broken," the commentator intoned, the stakes of the moment hanging heavily in the air.

As Zak began his descent the stadium fell into a hushed anticipation. He touched down with his skis carving into the snow—but the silence was soon filled with a murmur of disappointment.

The commentator's voice resonated with the crowd's sentiment,

"It's unfortunate—Zak's landing has not lived up to expectations."

In that fleeting moment the hopes of Zak reclaiming his spot atop the leaderboard and scoring a point dissipated like mist in the morning sun. His skis came to a stop and with them, the realization that his chance for redemption had slipped away on the unyielding ice. Zak Speed's journey in this ski jump event had ended, his dreams left shattered on the frozen slope.

Nearby in his camp 'Rohil' stood visibly anxious, stretching his limbs in preparation. His teammate, 'Unni' focused intently on polishing Rohil's skis to perfection. Komal, another team member approached with an iPad and handed it to Mysha, who was standing beside Rohil. Mysha scanned the data briefly before announcing,

"Wind speed at 20 km/h, precipitation at 0.5 milliliters. Conditions are perfect. Let's do this." With determination in their eyes, Rohil and Mysha made their way to the starting point.

The commentator continued with palpable excitement, *"This time, India has not one but two competitors in 'The Frozen Himalayan competition'. Our final contestant in the ski jumping event for the day is 'Rohil Dhoot'. Will he manage to break his compatriot Abeer Singh's record? We all must wait with bated breaths to see what would unfold"*

At the starting bar, Mysha looked at Rohil and offered a heartfelt, 'All the best'. With a nod, Rohil propelled himself down the slope.

The commentator's voice surged with energy, *"Cutting through the wind with precision, Rohil looks strong. His posture is flawless, easily the best we've seen so far. If he maintains this perfection through the jump, Abeer might be in trouble."*

As Rohil approached the take-off point, he bent his knees and leaped into the void with remarkable grace. Rohil descended fluidly, his form a picture of aerodynamics as his skis contacted snow.

But the snow betrayed him. It cracked, dragging Rohil several meters in a swirl of powdery snow.

"Oh no," Mysha gasped.

Judges hurried to the scene where Rohil stood in full gear. The large LCD screen replayed the footage in slow motion, scrutinizing the precise moment Rohil contacted the snow.

The commentator analyzed the situation and heightening tension among the crowd, remarked,

"We need to carefully determine the point of contact of Rohil's skis with the snow. The crack appeared about 3 meters past the k-line. If his landing point is exactly on the crack, Rohil will fall short of Abeer's distance point by mere centimeters. However, if it's beyond the crack, Rohil will take the lead. The judges are reviewing every frame meticulously."

After what felt like an eternity, the judges reached their verdict.

"It's unfortunate," declared the commentator, *"the judges have determined that Rohil's landing point is two centimeters behind Abeer's distance point. This means today's ski jump winner is Abeer, securing a crucial point and taking a lead in this very first ski jump event of the Frozen Himalyan competition 2023"*

A storm of fury and disappointment surged within Rohil. He flung his gear aside in a fit of rage.

"It's okay, Rohil," Mysha tried to calm him down.

But Rohil, consumed by frustration, shoved Mysha away and stormed off, declaring vehemently,

"A loss is a loss; it can never be okay.".

CHAPTER-2

THE CORPORATE MATRIX

Time flows ceaselessly forward, reshaping lives as it passes and Abeer's was no exception. Once a carefree child, he had settled seamlessly into the corporate grind, building a career in app development. The years had sculpted him into someone new—sharp, efficient, and controlled. Experience had cast an air of quiet seriousness over him, making him a man of few words but focused intent. His outlook had shifted and so had he.

Morning broke softly over the city the streets still drowsy in the pale light. Abeer navigated his car with practiced ease, the perfect knot of his corporate tie resting neatly against his crisp shirt. One hand rested lightly on the steering wheel while the other held a coffee tumbler. He sipped from it savoring the smooth bitterness of his cappuccino, a constant companion in the early hours. The silence in the car was broken by the melodic chime of his iPad. Without hesitation he tapped the screen and answered, his voice calm and professional,

"Good morning, this is Abeer Singh, Project Manager of the app development team. Welcome to 'App-logia', a company that creates apps and crafts the future." The words rolled off his tongue with ease, refined by habit. Within moments the conference call filled with voices—his colleagues from different corners of the world introducing themselves in a measured, professional cadence. For Abeer, it was just another start to another day.

By the time he pulled into the office parking lot, the city seemed to stretch awake around him though the building in front of him sat wrapped in calm stillness. The Bluetooth headset still nestled in his ear, he exited the car and strode toward the glass-front entrance of the office. His reflection followed him in the polished windows, mirroring his composed demeanour. He rode the elevator in silence, stepping into an empty floor where the hum of conversation and keyboards was yet to begin. With familiar ease, Abeer stopped at the biometric attendance machine resting his finger briefly against the cool glass before heading to his cabin—a space that was uniquely his own. Here, beneath the modern sheen of corporate precision, was another side to Abeer. Skis leaned in one corner, climbing ropes coiled neatly, an ice axe glinting faintly beneath the fluorescent lights. His gear felt alive, purposeful, ready. It was a small slice of adventure tucked into a world of deadlines and deliverables.

Every morning, this ritual grounded him. Before diving into the mountain of emails and sprints, he would take his time cleaning the equipment, his actions slow and deliberate. His calloused hands moved over skis and ropes brushing away dust like he was reconnecting with a part of himself buried beneath suits and spreadsheets. For Abeer, it wasn't just about preparation—it was a pause, a moment to remember who he was beyond the confines of the corporate machine. And no matter how crisp his shirts or how perfect his coffee, the climbing gear always whispered of something wilder—a life that he had left behind.

Fate has an uncanny way of bringing together people who seem destined to belong in entirely different worlds. Such was the case with Rohil and Abeer—two men who couldn't be more different if they tried.

During their college years, their paths never crossed. They were like two parallel lines, carving out lives that existed on separate planes. Yet, in the unpredictable dance of destiny, they both ended up at 'App-Logia', a burgeoning tech company, as project managers.

Rohil, the quintessential charmer with a magnetic personality, took the reins of the Design and User Experience (UX) team. His leadership style mirrored his personality—loud, dynamic, and overflowing with enthusiasm.

Abeer, in sharp contrast, moved with the precision of a clockwork machine, thriving in the quiet efficiency of his own methodical world. While Rohil basked in the spotlight, Abeer preferred to stay behind the scenes, letting his work speak louder than words.

Different as night and day, they now shared the same roof, their opposing styles destined to intertwine. Whether as rivals, co-workers or something else entirely, one thing was certain—Rohil and Abeer were two forces on a collision course, each one unknowingly drawn toward the other.

The office floor was alive that morning with the usual hum of activity—keyboards tapping in mismatched rhythms, phones buzzing and muted conversations creating a backdrop of organized chaos. Amidst it all, Rohil stormed in like a gust of wind, his entrance a performance in itself. Dressed in semi-formals with his carefree, messy hair somehow adding to his charisma. He exuded a loud confident energy that turned more than a few heads. He wasn't the kind of person you could miss—even if you tried. His team greeted him with a round of high-fives and laughter, their relaxed camaraderie bordering on friendship rather than mere professionalism. Rohil, the unofficial ringleader of the group gestured for everyone to assemble in the canteen. But before he could make it there, something made him stop.

Passing by Abeer's glass-walled cabin, his steps faltered and he cocked his head eyeing the man inside as though observing some fascinating new exhibit. Abeer sat at his desk, his posture rigid, eyes fixed on his computer screen with the kind of focus that bordered on obsessive.

"Oye Unni!" Rohil called over his shoulder, a blabbermouth and short in stature teammate, who had just caught up to him. *"When did this guy punch into the office today?"*

Unni followed Rohil's gaze to Abeer's cabin. *"He was there last night when I left the office,"* Unni informed him with playful seriousness. *"And when I cameback in the morning he was still there. Same chair, Same expression; working as if he has some looming deadline, though in reality none existed."*

Rohil tilted his head, thoroughly intrigued. *"Does this guy live in office or what?"* he asked, his lips twitching into a smirk. *"Go check under his *desk. Bet you'll find a mattress hidden somewhere."*

Both laughed, their amusement at Abeer's persistent work ethic loud enough to draw a faint glance from a nearby desk. Rohil shook his head in mock incredulity as he turned toward his own cabin. *"Of all the things,"* he muttered, half to himself referring to Abeer's working style, *"why does Abeer always have to jolt me like this?"*

Inside his cabin, Rohil made a casual flourish of throwing his iPad onto the desk and leaned back into his plush chair as if preparing for a royal decree. Unni lingered by the door before stepping in, clearly in the mood to continue the conversation.

"You know," Unni began, *"Abeer's probably the quietest person in this office. Guy rarely leaves his cabin, only ever talks about work and most of the time no one even knows he's here. So why,"* he asked, leaning against the desk, *"do you pay more attention to him than you do to us, your own team?"*

Rohil grinned lazily and placed a deliberate hand on Unni's shoulder, his taller frame making the gesture faintly condescending. *"Tell me something,"* Rohil said, his eyes gleaming mischievously. *"How do you know you're a man of compact frame?"* Refering to Unni's height.

Unni frowned, unsure where the conversation was going. He replied sheepishly *"Uh... by measuring my height?"*

Rohil shook his head like a teacher disappointed with a wrong answer. *"Measuring is unnecessary. Just come and stand next to me. It'll be obvious."*

Unni's smile faltered for just a moment, the sting of the barb evident in his eyes. He shot backward, stepping out of Rohil's reach, his face a picture of exaggerated caution. Rohil chuckled as he leaned back further, propping his feet on the corner of his desk in his signature casual style.

"Listen, your true potential isn't something you figure out on your own," Rohil said, his tone dropping into something more serious— for once. *"It shows when you manage to outperform someone who has*

same or better potential then you. Comparison draws conclusion that's how competition work."

Unni smirked, crossing his arms as if finally solving a great mystery. *"Ah!"* He said, pretending to stroke an invisible beard. *"So that's why you're always pitting Komal and me against each other, right? To bring out our true potential?"*

Rohil laughed and reached forward to pull Unni's cheeks in a patronizing gesture that Unni was all too familiar with—and hated.

"Exactly," Rohil said, grinning widely as Unni swatted his hands away. *"The stronger your opponent, the greater your success story becomes and, in this office, there's only one person better than Abeer."*

Unni raised an eyebrow, crossing his arms again. *"Here we go,"* he said, setting up Rohil's punchline with a theatrical flourish. *"And, of course, that person is..."*

"Me," Rohil finished with a dramatic point to himself, his grin triumphant.

Unni rolled his eyes but stepped closer, his voice growing more conspiratorial. *"Boss, if you weren't my boss..."* he began, deliberately leaving the sentence hanging.

Rohil sat up curious, his interest piqued. *"Alright then,"* he said, settling into a more relaxed stance. *"I'll give you two minutes. Pretend I'm not your boss—think of me as just another friend and speak what you intended to say, without any hesitation or fear."*

Taking the opportunity, Unni threw an arm around Rohil's shoulders, smirking and leaned in close like someone about to deliver the punchline to an inside joke. *"If you weren't my boss,"* Unni said slowly, with exaggerated sincerity, *"you'd be the biggest rascal I've ever met."*

For a moment, Rohil's grin vanished. He rolled his shoulder to shrug Unni's arm away with a slight jerk, his face suddenly serious. *"Your time's up,"* he said flatly.

Unni froze, genuinely unsure for a second if he'd taken the joke too far. *"Boss! You only gave me permission to express myself freely!"* he stuttered, his tone climbing into a slight panic. *"It's just a joke—there's no need to take offence!"*

Rohil's mask of seriousness cracked and a wide grin split his face before he burst into laughter, loud and unrestrained. *"The rascals who work under a rascal boss are even worse!"* he declared between fits of laughter. Unni relaxed as the tension evaporated, laughing along with him and for a moment, their shared humor rippled through the cabin.

But as the laughter faded, Rohil glanced out of the glass wall of his cabin, his gaze lingering on Abeer's door. His tone softened again, losing the lightness from earlier. *"You know,"* Rohil said quietly, almost to himself, *"the real thrill of success isn't just achieving it. It's when even your biggest competitor appreciates it."*

Unni followed his gaze but didn't push further. Rohil let that statement settle for a moment then shook off his reflective mood and smacked Unni on the back. *"Let's go, champ. Time to head to the canteen."*

And with that, Rohil marched out of his office cabin, leading Unni like a general heading into battle—or, in this case, breakfast. Behind them, the steady hum of the office continued but something hung heavier in the air—the quiet kind of rivalry that could either breed bitterness or perhaps, something better.

The office canteen teemed with chatter and laughter as Rohil's team gathered in an informal circle around the central table. The star of the moment wasn't human. It was a tray of small shot glasses filled with vibrant green gourd juice, each topped with a light dusting of black salt like a chef's finishing flourish. Komal, the self-proclaimed "juice sommelier," stood proudly by the tray, her expression suggesting she was unveiling some kind of elixir for immortality instead of mere vegetable pulp.

The double doors swung open, and in strode Rohil with his usual mix of easy confidence and sly charm, accompanied by his steadfast wingman, Unni. Catching sight of Komal's display, Rohil grinned as though he'd just encountered a long-lost friend.

"Komal," he said, eyes gleaming with anticipation, *"are we ready for this?"*

"Ready and black-salted to perfection," Komal replied, crossing her arms with mock seriousness.

Rohil clapped his hands together. *"Black salt? That's what separates amateurs from professionals. You've outdone yourself."*

As if on cue, every team member aligned themselves with a shot glass in hand. Rohil raised his own and said with commanding lightness,

"Alright, team. On my count. One, two... go!"

In unison, twenty shot glasses tipped back. The juice went down with varying receptions: some groaned, some laughed, others simply grimaced. But it wasn't until 'Shitendu' a.k.a 'Shit' staggered back looking like he'd taken a blow, seeing him the team broke into outright laughter. The visibly pale-faced Shitendu plopped into a chair shaking his head in dismay.

Unni smirked and leaned toward Rohil. *"Pretty sure Shit tapped out."*

Rohil glanced at his dazed colleague with mock concern. *"Shit, what's wrong? I've never seen gourd juice hit someone this hard."*

Shitendu let out a long-suffering sigh, his head cradled in his hands. *"It's last night's party. I feel like I've been hanging upside-down ever since. That was a mistake, never again."* He exhaled, half in regret, half in defiance.

Rohil crouched beside him, his grin turning sly. *"Look, my friend, let me teach you something about the professional world. The team that drinks together, sticks together. It's not about what you're drinking—it's about the bond. Call it a ritual! Now go on, soldier... another shot will make you stronger."*

Before Shitendu could respond a voice cut through the canteen like a whip. *"Rohil."*

The mood shifted at once. Conversations died mid-sentence, laughter evaporated and twenty heads turned toward the entrance. Standing there, framed by the light of the corridor behind him was Gautam—the Chief Technology Officer of App-Logia, a man whose mere presence could make keyboards type faster and silence conversations mid-thought. His sharp gaze barely skimmed over the others before locking on Rohil.

"Good morning, Gautam sir!" came the collective, sheepish greeting from the group.

"Good morning," Gautam replied curtly, his voice heavy with the kind of professionalism that could drain all colour from a room. Then, his focus zeroed in on Rohil.

"Mr. Rohil Dhoot, if your little… bonding exercise is over, perhaps you could direct your attention toward some actual work?" Gautam commanded with sarcasm.

Rohil straightened at once, silently cursing his luck but offering his best smile. *"Absolutely, sir. Right away."*

Gautam gave the group a dismissive look before walking off. His shoes tapping out an authoritative rhythm on the elegant floor. Rohil quickly followed him, falling into step as they moved through the corridor toward the meeting room.

"Sir," Rohil ventured cautiously, still trying to gauge Gautam's current mood. *"If I may ask, what's today's meeting about?"*

The CTO's eyes remained fixed ahead. *"I don't know—why don't you tell me? Didn't you read the email?"*

Caught off-guard but unwilling to admit defeat, Rohil cleared his throat. *"I did, sir, but, uh… I couldn't quite figure out why our CEO (Chief executive officer) Mr. Harish Brown is suddenly in India on such short notice."*

At this, Gautam slowed his pace slightly, finally turning to give Rohil a cold unreadable look. *"You'll find out in the meeting,"* he said quietly, then added, almost as an afterthought, *"provided you manage to stay for the entire discussion."*

Rohil smiled tightly, sensing an edge in the words but unwilling to play into it. *"Don't worry, sir. I'll be on my A-game. Hard work all the way."*

Gautam's lips twitched slightly though whether it was amusement or disdain was unclear. *"Hmm. That's good to hear. Because, as far as I'm aware, salaries are paid for work not for throwing back shots of gourd juice."*

Rohil winced inwardly but offered nothing more than a sheepish, *"Right, sir."*

As the CTO strode ahead, leaving him to trail behind. In the silence of the corridor, Rohil could nearly hear his own thoughts teasing him:

"Looks like today, gourd juice wasn't the hardest thing to swallow after all. Gautam is even more bitter"

The conference room was a hive of energy filled with an unspoken urgency as the team settled into their seats. At the head of the oval table stood Mr. Harish Brown, the CEO with an air of quiet authority. His mixed heritage – half Indian, half American – reflected not just in his appearance but also in his ability to seamlessly balance tradition with a sharp business sense. Dressed in his signature tailored suit, he radiated confidence as he greeted the room.

"Good morning, everyone," Harish said, his commanding voice breaking the subdued hum of the room.

"Good morning, Harish," came the synchronized response from the team.

Gautam, Abeer, and Rohil were seated alongside other members, all ready for the challenge that lay ahead. Harish caught Gautam's glance and gave a subtle nod, signaling him to take over. Gautam, the poised strategist leaned forward with the faintest hint of a smile on his lips as he began.

"Creating apps isn't just our job—it's our passion," Gautam said, his words carrying the ease of someone who had done this countless times yet still found excitement in every new project. He continued, *"It's something we excel at because it's a craft we've spent years perfecting. But let me state the obvious—bringing new clients onboard isn't easy. It's a constant battle. There are always cut-rate developers out there, overpromising at absurdly low prices, leaving clients with half-baked solutions. Our job is to ensure clients see the value of quality in our work, the risks of shortcuts and the importance of doing it right the first time. That becomes even more critical when we step into uncharted territory."*

Harish, always quick to seize an opportunity leaned forward slightly, his fingers folded together. *"Especially,"* he interjected smoothly, *"when our reputation is on the line."* His tone was serious yet charged with possibility. *"Sports tourism is one of the fastest-growing trends in the travel industry right now. And we've had the good fortune to land a project that's both exciting and challenging. We've been chosen to create a sports tourism app for an iconic brand—India's oldest and most respected sports goods manufacturer, 'Savi Sports'. It's a powerhouse that has been around since 1801."*

The statement lingered in the room, the weight of the project filling the air. Even for a team accustomed to high-pressure assignments this one felt monumental, as they had never developed a sports app before. Harish's eyes glinted as he continued, the personal connection in his voice unmistakable. *"This project is particularly close to my heart. Savi Sports is a legacy brand and its owners are close family friends. Their forefathers built this company and now their next generation wants to take it in a bold new direction. The plan is to expand into sports tourism—not just across India, but globally."*

Gautam stepped back into the conversation as if choreographed.

"Savi Sports has an incredible history," he said, his voice calm but filled with admiration. *"They started out handcrafting cricket bats for British players during the colonial era. Over two centuries later they've become a name synonymous with sports manufacturing. But the*

new generation sees the big picture—they want to build more than just products. They want to create experiences. And that's where we come in."

Harish nodded approvingly, his sharp gaze sweeping over the table.

"Let me make this clear," Harish said, his tone inspiring yet firm. *"This app needs to be more than a digital tool. It has to be a transformative experience that reflects the excellence of the Savi Sports brand. We're not just creating functionality here—we're crafting a doorway into the future of their business. And that means we're going to be working hard. Research, late nights, prototypes—whatever it takes. We are aiming for nothing less than the best sports tourism app in the world."*

There was a ripple of energy in the room, a collective acknowledgment of the challenge ahead. Gautam stepped in again, playing the role of the team's orchestrator. *"Here's how we'll break this down,"* he began authoritatively. *"Abeer, you and your team will handle both the front- and back-end development. Rohil, you'll take charge of the overall design and user experience—the UI and UX must be spot on."*

Abeer, who'd been intently listening, raised a hand to chime in.

"Can I just add something here?" he began, a spark of excitement lighting up his voice. *"I've been thinking about how we can expand the scope of the app. You know the old saying, 'killing two birds with one stone'? I think it's outdated. Today, the real trick isn't just hitting two targets—it's hitting every target in a single shot. Why not make that our approach?"*

Gautam tilted his head, intrigued but unsure where Abeer was headed. *"Explain,"* he said simply.

Abeer bent forward, the idea building as he spoke. *"Savi Sports already has a great reputation and the kind of network that we can leverage. They've got stores and distribution centres all over the country. Why not include a section in the app for sports quick commerce? Q-commerce is booming right now—speed is everything. Imagine the app not only helping with sports tourism but also serving as a platform for instantly delivering sports goods and equipment. This could give Savi Sports an edge they never even imagined."*

The meeting had begun to crackle with energy, and the room carried an undercurrent of tension as Abeer's bold suggestion about incorporating q-commerce into the app stirred debate. Abeer had been calm yet firm, passionately defending his idea but it didn't sit well with everyone.

Up until now, Rohil had been listening quietly, his face a practiced mask of neutrality. But when Abeer leaned into his argument laying out his vision with confidence, Rohil straightened in his chair ready to challenge it. With a smirk that betrayed an edge of mockery, he spoke up his tone casual but cutting. *"Abeer, your smart idea of hitting multiple targets with a single shot will destroy the entire app development business."*

The laughter from Rohil's team that followed his jab at Abeer lingered for a moment but Rohil wasn't one to leave his argument half-baked. He levelled in his chair, his smirk fading into a look of seriousness. Leaning forward, he fixed his gaze on Abeer. His voice cutting through the room like a sharp edge.

"Abeer, you're not just trying to mix two entirely distinct business models—you're risking complete chaos. By merging two vastly different concepts into one app, you're diluting the essence of both and sabotaging what could be two separate success stories. Think about it— sports tourism is its own specialized market and q-commerce is an entirely different beast. Combining them doesn't just confuse the purpose—it also kills our chance to pitch for two contracts, two apps that could each stand out on their own."

Abeer stooped ahead, his posture calm but his voice carrying an unmistakable fire.

"I think Rohil is overlooking something critical here. Visibility," he said simply but firmly. *"Sports tourism is a fantastic idea and when it works, yes, the margins will be huge for the client. But what about the off-season? What about the lean times when there are no tourists and less activity? Who do we rely on to keep the business running then? An app like this can't afford to stagnate for months. By integrating q-commerce we ensure that the app is relevant and functional year-round.*

Sports goods don't have an off-season—they're always in demand. This addition doesn't distract from the app's core purpose—it keeps it alive."

The room shifted slightly—some faces lit with interest others still skeptical. Sensing the need to drive his argument home, Abeer pulled out his phone and held it up, weaving a story that turned every set of eyes onto him.

"Picture this," he said, his voice growing more animated. "It's the middle of the night, you're at a friend's get-together, and someone suddenly suggests playing cards. Everyone's excited but there's just one problem—the host can't find their deck of cards. It's a small need, sure but frustrating. Now imagine pulling out our app. You tap a button and within ten minutes those cards are delivered right to your doorstep. Problem solved, instantly. The app doesn't just stay relevant—it transforms into their everyday companion, reliable and indispensable."

The room was quiet for a beat and then the murmurs started. Abeer had managed to breathe life into his concept, giving the team a tangible vision of how sports q-commerce could work.

Gautam, seated next to Harish, smiled and said, *"Sir, this is a wonderful plan."* Harish nodded; his expression thoughtful. *"Great idea. Let's develop this app as quickly as possible,"* he said decisively, glancing at Gautam in agreement.

But while satisfaction rippled across the room, not everyone felt triumphant. Rohil forced a tight smile although his frustration was evident. There was a flicker of something else in his eyes—pride or was it defiance? hunching ahead, Rohil addressed Harish directly.

"Sir, back in college, I was already working on an app for adventure sports. I had the whole thing conceptualised—it could have been huge. But when funding fell through, the project stalled. That doesn't mean I forgot what I learned. You'll see—my team will make this app extraordinary. Trust me."

His words were layered with more than just determination; they carried an undercurrent of rivalry that wasn't lost on anyone in the room. Harish nodded but his gaze flicked between Abeer and Rohil.

The tension between Abeer and Rohil remained unspoken but undeniable. Harish, though outwardly calm, couldn't ignore the fire in their eyes. He knew that this rivalry, while intense, could also be the key to pushing the entire team toward excellence. Knowing this made him smile faintly. Out of conflict comes innovation, he thought. And soon enough, Savi Sports would have an app that reflected not just their vision but the unyielding drive of the individuals building it. The quiet battle between Abeer and Rohil, it seemed, had just begun.

At the sports arena within App-Logia—an office that prided itself on its work-life balance; Abeer was immersed in an intense game of table tennis with his subordinate, Amit. Each of Abeer's sharp precise shots carried an air of tension, a reflection of the swirling unspoken thoughts within him. His focus was obstinate, his eyes unblinking, as though winning this game might free him from an unseen burden. Meanwhile, Rohil strolled into the area with Unni. Casually picking up a racket, he leaned on the edge of the table watching the game, biding his turn.

Suddenly Amit's phone rang and he stepped aside to answer the call. With no one to face him, Abeer sent another fiery shot across the table—only for Rohil to instinctively return it. What started as a quick reflex turned into an electrifying rally. Abeer and Rohil faced off with an intensity that belied the casual setting. Each shot came faster, stronger, the ping of the ball echoing through the sports arena like a battle cry. Sweat poured down their faces as they played on incessantly. Their blazing strokes feeling like an impromptu boxing match with fists of rubber and wood. The few onlookers including Unni and Amit watched in awe, captivated as neither player showed any signs of slowing.

Finally, Amit stepped in catching the ball mid-flight and breaking the spell of the endless rally. *"Abeer,"* he said firmly, *"it's time for the meeting."* That simple statement grounded Abeer, pulling him out of the game and back into reality. Frustration flickered across his face as he turned and set the paddle down. His heavy steps as he walked away spoke volumes; it was as though he carried a weight far beyond just anger.

Rohil wasn't one to let such a moment pass without a jab. *"Mr. Sportsman,"* he called out smugly, *"why don't we settle the score sometime? Saturday evening game, maybe?"* *The jab hit a nerve.*

Already simmering from Rohil's earlier sarcastic remarks in the meeting room, Abeer spun around, his anger spilling over in a rare outburst,

"You're nothing but a fake player," he said sharply. *"Playing video games doesn't make you an athlete. A real sportsman lives every second of their life for sports—dedicated to the game, to the discipline and to the grind. You'll never know what it takes."*

Rohil smirked, unshaken by Abeer's accusation, and threw back his usual brand of pointed humour. He slyly replied,

"If a player is the oxygen that flows into the lungs, then an opponent is the carbon dioxide—that crucial but dirty element. And honestly, you won't find an opponent better than me."
Abeer dismissed Rohil's comment with a direct accusation,

"You're intimidated by me."

Rohil took the insult in stride, turning it into another sarcastic jab:

"Maybe you're right. I am cautious of you, having you as a rival is my best motivation to push harder to remain on the top."

Abeer said nothing. His silence spoke the loudest and without another glance he turned and walked away completely tuned out to Rohil's presence. And in many ways his indifference, an utter refusal to further engage in a spat, stung Rohil more than any retort could have.

As Abeer disappeared down the hall, Rohil stood by the table tapping the paddle on his open palm. A sly grin lingered on his face as he muttered under his breath, *"Tough nut. I like it."* With that he set the racket down.

As Rohil strolled out of the sports arena, he noticed Unni lingering behind, his stance hesitant, his eyes still following him. Rohil stopped in his tracks, turned around and smirked. *"What's the matter?"* he teased, his voice dripping with humor. *"Don't tell me you're standing there admiring me like I'm your long-lost girlfriend or something."*

Unni scoffed at the remark but couldn't quite let the moment slide. *"We never finished our last game of ping-pong,"* he said firmly, folding his arms across his chest. *"* **Let's get this settled today.** *"*

Rohil raised an eyebrow, clearly amused by the challenge but shrugged with a theatrical air of disinterest. *"After playing with Abeer, anyone else just feels... dull."* He waved his hand as if brushing the suggestion away, already turning back toward the exit.

That earned a sharp glare from Unni who instantly straightened and stepped forward, unwilling to let Rohil get away with undermining him. *"For your information (FYI),"* Unni shot back, his voice lined with pride, *"I'm a national-level table tennis player. I'm better than Abeer and I'll prove it anytime, anywhere."*

Rohil came to an abrupt halt and for a moment Unni thought his words had sunk in. Instead, Rohil turned an exaggerated expression of mock-sympathy on his face. He placed a hand on Unni's shoulder and grinned, his tone dripping with sarcasm.

"Better than Abeer, huh? Alright... but at least leave me some motivation to comeback for my next life. If I'm already surrounded by greatness in this lifetime then what's there to look forward to after reincarnation?" Rohil laughed as if he'd delivered the best punchline of the century.

Unni clenched his jaw not appreciating Rohil's bold proclamation but before he could respond Rohil tugged him along like one might an old friend, his tone light and carefree again.

"No worries," Rohil said with a smile, his teasing continuing. *"Just practice hard in this life. By the time your next one comes around, you might finally be good enough to stand a chance against me."*

His laughter echoed down the hallway as they walked away together with the lingering frustration on Unni's face and the fire in his eyes

FRACTURED TIES

The morning was biting cold, the kind that clung to the air and froze the breath mid-motion. Fog hung heavy curling across the training ground like a veil but Abeer emerged through it—a figure of quiet purpose, running steadily in his tracksuit. His strides were firm, unyielding and focused; as though the wind, the chill, even time itself couldn't slow him.

Behind him trailed another figure—Neet, elegant yet equally persistent, her movements a mirror of his. She matched his pace, her presence unshakable. Her eyes fixed on him with a mix of determination and frustration.

Abeer didn't need to turn to know she was following him—he felt her presence like a shadow—but he gave her nothing. No reaction, no acknowledgment. With each push-up and dip, she followed at a distance matching his efforts but always staying just far enough away to be ignored.

With the crash mat strapped to his back, Abeer soon set his sights on a towering boulder at the far end of the field. He approached it, his piercing gaze locked on its rough face and began to climb without a word. Neet, unshaken by his silence positioned herself below the boulder. Her arms raised to guide him onto the crash mat should any misstep pull him down. She stayed steady, ready, her concern evident but Abeer's indifference remained—steadfast and unabating.

Once done, Abeer slipped the mat over his shoulder and began the familiar walk home. His figure disappearing into the remnants of fog. Neet followed him, her resolve seemingly unbreakable despite his quietude. She trailed him all the way to the bungalow where Abeer bent to pick up the morning newspaper, barely looking up as he slipped through the gate. For a moment, Neet stared at the gate her frustration simmering behind her calm expression. But she wasn't ready to leave—not yet.

Just then, Sunita, Abeer's mother, called out from her chair in the garden, her soft voice breaking the quiet.

"Neet! Oh, dear, when did you arrive? Have you finished your mountaineering certification?" Sunita took a sip of her tea, the distant warmth of her former liveliness flickering faintly. Her smile though kind

didn't hide the weariness hidden behind it.

Neet, turned to face her and nearly exploded, frustration finally breaking free as she complains,

"It was difficult to finish it without Abeer! Three years—three years—and not one call, not one message. Whenever I called, he'd just say 'I'm busy' and hang up! Every single time!" Her voice trembled slightly—not just with anger but with hurt.

Sunita sighed softly. Time had worn down the bold, confident edge she used to wear like armour, leaving a quieter, gentler version of herself behind. *"He's so different now,"* she said, her eyes dropping to her teacup. *"Since he gave up mountaineering, it's like he's locked himself away from everyone… even from me."*

Neet shook her head the anger in her voice now replaced with something softer, something almost pleading. *"Fine,"* she said, *"if he has problems with himself, I understand. But why did he stop talking to me? What did I do wrong?"*

Sunita's gaze met hers, full of meaning but without an answer. She sighed again, helpless. *"That's something only Abeer can justify."*

Neet's, voice raising with fire again. *"Alright,"* she said, *"then I'll ask him. Right away."* annoyance burned in her tone as she turned toward the entrance door.

Sunita reached out trying to calm her. *"Neet,"* she said softly, *"he's been getting better, slowly. App-Logia job has helped. At least he's leaving the house now."*

Neet paused, looking directly into Sunita's tired eyes. *"But is he happy with what he is doing?"* The question shattered whatever pretence Sunita might have been trying to hold, leaving a weighty silence in its place. Sunita looked down, unable to answer.

Rolling her eyes in exasperation Neet turned and walked away, her footsteps falling heavy on the garden path. Sunita remained behind alone in her thoughts. She let out a whisper barely audible in the cold air. *"Maybe it's my fault,"* she murmured, her voice tinged with regret,

"Maybe I should have let him chase his dreams."

As the morning wind swirled around her, she took another sip of tea though the warmth no longer reached her.

Morning light seeped through the blinds as Neet stepped into Abeer's room, her eyes immediately locking onto the collage on his wall. It was a tapestry of frozen memories—pictures of them scaling cliffs, rafting through roaring waters and caught in moments that whispered of tenderness and love. The collage seemed out of place now, relics of a past that no longer aligned with the world they both currently inhabited. Neet's jaw clenched, her gaze turned sharp and resolute though there was a faint glimmer of something softer beneath her defiance. Just then the sound of a door opening pulled her attention.

Abeer emerged from the bathroom, a towel slung casually around his waist and water droplets trailing down his shoulders. He barely acknowledged Neet as he strode to the mirror, picking up a comb. His movements were mechanical, precise and his dark eyes flicked briefly to Neet's reflection within the glass before he resumed fixing his hair. Neet, however, didn't look away from the collage. Her voice broke the quiet cutting through the space between them, laced with a mix of irony and command.

"Why are you still here? Come with me." Her gaze lingering on the collage and her words heavy with subtext. It was almost as if she were addressing the collection of photos and memories on the wall—or perhaps to the version of herself hidden among its fragments.

Determined, she stepped closer to the collage, her fingers curling around its edges as she tugged but it didn't budge. Her frustration only deepened as Abeer, calm and immovable spoke without turning towards her,

"If you pull the wrong way, the frame will break."

"So let it break." Neet voice was a razor-edged whisper, her teeth grinding as she yanked harder. *"I'll make do with the pieces."*

With one final pull the collage came loose and Neet held it in her hands. For a moment her expression softened as her eyes fell on a photo of them at the edge of a mountaintop, the sun rising behind them. Both looked exhilarated and alive. She traced the contours of that memory with her gaze before her voice cut through again, sharp as a knife.

"Climbing is our life," Neet said, as if daring Abeer to deny it.

Abeer didn't flinch. Slowly he buttoned his shirt looking through her, lost in thought. Finally, he replied, his tone blunt and flat.

"It's the truth of your life. Not mine."

The words struck her but she didn't give him the satisfaction of letting him see it. Instead, she stormed toward him thrusting the collage out like it was something toxic.

"Then take it," she snapped. *"If it's not your life, throw it away. Dump it in the trash where it belongs."*

But Abeer didn't reach for it. He didn't even look at it. He carried on dressing with that same maddening calm, as though her voice couldn't pierce the invisible armor, he'd wrapped himself in. And yet, in that very silence she could feel it—the unspoken heaviness that hung between them like a shadow refusing to leave.

"You stopped answering my calls and never bothered to return them," she said, voice quieter, almost trembling now. *"So, what does that mean? That I don't matter to you anymore? Or worse... that you've grown to despise me?"*

Abeer froze for half a beat before exhaling audibly, the barest sign of frustration bleeding through. His voice emerged flat but weighted, as if every syllable had been carefully considered in advance.

"I didn't stop calling because I hate you, Neet."

It wasn't enough. A crack opened in her carefully held composure. She stepped closer, her determination undiminished.

"Then what?" she demanded. *"What's this? Are we even in a relationship anymore?"* Her voice turned soft but bitter, biting down on the vulnerability threatening to spill out. *"What would you even call this relationship? A—"* she paused, smirking bitterly at her own words— "A **ghost relationship that lingers in the background, stuck in pause mode.**"

The sarcastic term hovered in the air, unanswered. Abeer was silent still fastening his trousers. He deliberately avoided meeting her gaze, as if locking eyes with her would unleash the Pandora's box of emotions he was desperate to keep sealed. The quiet between them grew too loud, pressing against her until it became unbearable. And then, like a dam breaking beneath the weight of all the years they hadn't spoken, the truth tumbled out of Neet.

"Three years, Abeer," her voice cracked with emotion. *"Three years and not one call. Don't you think I deserve an answer for that? Why?"*

He didn't hesitate this time. The response came swift, clear and as sharp as a knife he'd kept unsheathed inside him for far too long.

"I didn't call you because I didn't want technologist Abeer to fall apart."

Her frustration flared again but now there was a flicker of something tender—concern mingling with the confusion that seemed ready to erupt. *"Technologist Abeer?"* she echoed.

"Yes," he continued, his voice sharper now, tinged with a rare vulnerability. *"Talking to you meant reminding myself of 'climber Abeer in me'. It meant feeling the weight of everything I gave up. And every time I felt that the climber in me would rear up, grab the techie in me by the throat and scream, run away from here. This isn't you—you're not meant to be trapped in some glossy corporate office. You're meant for*

the mountains, for the wild, where you truly come alive." He finally turned to look at her, his eyes aflame with the raw agony he'd buried for years. *"Every time I heard your voice, I knew you were pursuing our dream while I stayed behind staring at sprints and prototypes telling myself it was the right thing for me to do."*

The weight of his confession hung in the air between them. For so long, Neet had imagined the silence between them to be indifference. Now, hearing the truth she saw it for what it was—a war he'd been fighting within himself. Over the years, Abeer had trained himself to view life through a lens of pessimism, convincing himself that the truth only brought sharper and darker edges to reality. After brief introspection he spoke again, his voice heavy and grim.

"When Dad died, the balance in his account was 500 rupees. That's the truth of a seasoned and professional mountaineer's life, Neet. Now tell me—how am I supposed to bury that truth?" His words weren't just a reflection of his pain; they revealed the cracks in the façade he had carefully constructed. He didn't want pity or hope, or lectures. He wanted this conversation to just end.

But Neet wasn't one to give in easily. It wasn't her way—just like it wasn't her way to bow down to obstacles or walk away from the mountains she was drawn to conquer.

"Come on, Abeer." Her voice carried an urgency, an undercurrent of belief that cut through his bitterness. *"How can you even begin to compare passion with money?"*

Abeer didn't answer immediately. Instead, he turned toward his cupboard, pulled out a tie and began knotting it with a mechanical precision that spoke more about his resignation than calm. Tying that tie was his shield, his ritual of putting the corporate mask back on. After a moment he finally spoke and while his tone was measured, his words were tangled with intensity.

"I made a trade, Neet. I compromised my passion for money. And it was a very expensive deal. It took a lot of effort but I finally got my passion to quiet down. It's buried now and I've made my peace with that."

Neet watched him as he spoke and it became clear to her that he wasn't at peace at all. What he called peace looked more like a truce—fragile, temporary and bound to break. He might have convinced himself that he could live this half-life forever but she knew compromises like these had limits. His corporate façade could only hold steady for so long before it began to crumble under the sheer weight of his unlived dreams. And so, she pushed harder this time going straight for where it hurt the most—his ego. She didn't flinch when she said,

"You're a loser, Abeer."

Her voice was even, almost detached but her words hit the core of him. She saw it in the way his hands froze for just a second before resuming the knot on his tie. She pressed on, cutting deeper. *"You know Abeer, being a climber isn't easy—it's physically, mentally, and socially daunting, especially for an orphan like me. But that doesn't mean I stop. Just because the path is harder doesn't mean I abandon it halfway. Every step leads somewhere and that's more than what I can say for sitting where you are now."*

Abeer's jaw clenched. He knew exactly what she was doing—steering the conversation to places he swore he wouldn't go, digging at the parts of himself he'd refused to confront. He wasn't going to let her pull him back into a life he had spent years trying to bury. *"Neet,"* he said firmly, his sharp tone cutting through the tension. *"You're not wrong. I'm not wrong. We just have different priorities."* His eyes met hers for the briefest moment but the finality in his voice was unmistakable.

"This argument ends here."

Neet felt the walls go up around him again, thicker and higher than before and for the first time her resolve wavered. She had come here ready to fight for him but what was the point of fighting if his mind was already closed? And yet, the part of her that refused to give up whispered that there was still a chance—there had to be. Her voice broke slightly as she said, softer now,

"At least try, Abeer. Please."

His response was immediate, cold, and unflinching. *"There's no point,*

Neet," he said. *"The ropes that connected techie Abeer and Climber Abeer—they're all broken now."* He turned away from her before she could respond, before he could see the tears welling up in her eyes. Her lips parted but no words came and at that moment the air between them felt thicker than it ever had before. Abeer didn't face her again, afraid of what her expression might do to his carefully controlled emotions. Instead, he deflected his voice softening with a pinch of tenderness she wasn't expecting.

"Mom made your favorite Muli (radish) parathas," he said, still with his back to her. *"Have some before you leave."*

There it was—an echo of the affection that still lingered between them, even if he wouldn't—or couldn't—acknowledge it. Without another word he picked up his bag and walked out, leaving silence in his wake. Neet stood there frozen in place, as few tears slipped down her cheeks. She fought them off, refusing to let the moment break her completely. But deep down, for the first time she wondered if Abeer was already too far gone. If her words, no matter how true or sharp could ever reach the part of him he'd buried alongside his dreams.

COLLATERAL FLIRTATION

The office floor at App-Logia was a tale of two worlds. Where on one side, Rohil's team thrived in a vibrant laid-back workspace filled with beanbags, low couches, and capsule pods for quick escapes—a reflection of their easy-going inventive approach to work. On the other side was Abeer's team, enclosed in an orderly grid of desks and austere corporate furniture, embodying a no-nonsense disciplined ethos. The stark visual split wasn't just a design choice but a statement—a physical representation of two distinct attitudes toward professionalism and pleasure.

Inside Rohil's cabin, the 'Savi Sports' App development meeting was in full swing. A lively discussion on structure and functionality buzzed among the team. Rohil, always comfortable leading such creative huddles, delegated responsibilities with enthusiasm. Unni, whose technical grasp of UX was unmatched, was handed the task of research, wire-framing, and prototyping while the app's visual heart—the UI—would rest in the hands of Mysha.

But Mysha, a star designer known as much for her sharp mind as her striking presence was noticeably missing from the meeting. Rohil was about to mention her absence, just then the doors to the room flung open and in she walked with her usual flair, a mix of charm and confidence that instantly changed the energy in the room. For a moment, Rohil, who prided himself on composure faltered. His words hesitated on the edge of his lips while his eyes betrayed a fondness for Mysha, which he never quite managed to hide. As if on cue, his tone shifted; the sharp, focused leader softened into someone irresistibly drawn into Mysha's orbit.

"The air in this office always changes the moment you step in, Mysha." Rohil quipped, the smile in his voice unmistakable.

Without missing a beat, Mysha fired back, her wit always setting a new standard for their playful exchanges.

"Well, maybe I can't change you, but at least I can manage to change the air around you."

Her retort earned a chorus of laughter from the team. It was always like this when the two of them sparred—a dynamic that blurred the line between professionalism and flirtation. Not one to back down, Rohil leaned closer, his voice dropping just for her.

"Tone down the perfume of yours," he teased with a hint of mock possessiveness. *"I don't want your scent attracting anyone else in office but me."*

Mysha raised an eyebrow, the corners of her lips lifting in playful defiance.

"Without commitment, there are no guarantees to hold on," she teased, her words laced with subtle playful smirk on her lips.

Rohil chuckled knowingly. *"Commitment in a relationship?"* he said. *"That's for people who lack trust in themselves."*

Effortlessly, Mysha shifted the focus back to the room, her footsteps carrying her toward the projector.

"If I didn't trust you," she said, her voice measured and calm, *"I'd have never agreed to share an apartment with you in this unfamiliar city."*

Her words hung in the air, validating their unique equation but leaving just enough room for speculation. Rohil, never one to let her have the final word leaned back in his chair with a teasing smile.

"You're lucky to be in a live-in relationship with someone like me," he said with mock arrogance before shifting his gaze toward Komal. *"Just look at Komal—poor thing's been waiting for months to move in with her boyfriend but the guy's unable to take the leap."*

Komal, clearly unimpressed with being dragged into their verbal jousting, straightened in her seat and directed a pointed look at Rohil. *"Actually,"* she started, her voice crisp and cutting, *"Gautam sir is way ahead of you Rohil. That's why he gave the UI team permanent work-from-home schedules,"* she said looking at Mysha. *"He probably knew that if you two ever worked regularly in the same space, the entire office would collapse under the weight of your endless flirting."*

The meeting room hummed with lighthearted chatter as Unni leaned back and took a shot at Komal, unable to resist a playful dig. *"Decorum, huh?"* he smirked. *"Coming from someone whose social calendar is busier than her work schedule."* The group burst into laughter.

Rohil didn't enjoy seeing his team turning the meeting into a comedy club, especially when the jokes were close to home. His jaw tightened, the playful Rohil giving way to the more serious work-mode version of himself. *"Guys! We're here for a meeting,"* he said sharply, his tone cutting through the laughter, *"not to mess around."*

But Mysha, who knew exactly how to press his buttons, wasn't about to let it slide. She tilted her head, her voice mock-sweet yet sharp as a blade.

"If it was a meeting, you could have just come, made your point, and left. Who asked you to start poking at people? **Keep poking, and you'll find yourself drowning in a flood of mocks. Karma, Rohil—what you dish out always comes back around."**

A ripple of cheerful chuckles spread through the room but before Rohil could respond, the women in the room rose to their feet, rallying around Mysha with exaggerated solidarity. *"This is so unfair, Rohil,"* one of them chimed in. *"When you joke it's all good fun but when we say anything it's suddenly changes to a waste of time?"* Mysha stood at the centre of the small rebellion with her arms crossed there was a satisfied smirk on her face as she raised a single brow at Rohil.

The room erupted into applause and laughter at their remark, however Rohil's face hardened into an expression of boss-like authority cutting through the chaos with a single gesture,

"Alright, enough," he said, his sharp tone instantly silencing the room. *"I need top-quality output from everyone. The kind of work that not only matches but outshines Abeer's team's front and back-end development. No more messing around. Let's get down to business."*

It was always fascinating to watch Rohil switch gears. One moment, he was the easygoing guy who could laugh and banter with the best of them; the next, he was a leader who brooked no nonsense and demanded nothing less than excellence. It was that duality—his charm and his intensity—that gave him such sway over his team.

The group settled back into their seats and the air in the room shifted as Mysha stepped up to present her vision for the 'Savi Sports' app. With an effortless confidence she began outlining her concept: a sleek, sports-centric design that combined bold visuals with seamless usability. From the stylish, consistent buttons to the vibrant color scheme that echoed the brand's legacy, to typography that felt dynamic yet readable, every choice Mysha made seemed deliberate and inspired. The way she articulated her ideas—her acute attention to detail, her ability to bring clarity and aesthetics into perfect harmony—left the room silent in awe.

Rohil sat back in his chair watching her intently, the corners of his mouth twitching in what could have been a smile though his expression was harder to read. Mysha's talent was unmatched and she proved it time and again. Even working remotely, she achieved what an entire team would have struggled to create together. It was this brilliance that had put her leagues ahead of others in her field—but for Rohil, it was more than just her professional genius. There was something magnetic about her, the way she controlled the room while staying utterly herself, unflinching and unapologetic.

It was in moments like these he couldn't help but remember why she was so much more than just another teammate to him, why he couldn't quite meet her teasing gaze without the faintest flicker of something deeper passing through his own. Mysha wasn't just beautiful, she was extraordinary—and Rohil could do nothing but stare, privately marvelling at how utterly she drew him in despite how fiercely he tried to resist it.

The meeting room's chaos settled as focus tightened. Rohil led the core team to his cabin, leaving the noise behind. In the quiet decisions began to take shape, where ideas could breathe.

Rohil leaned back in his chair lost in the flow of the intense discussion with his core team—Unni, Mysha, and Komal—when across the glass walls of his cabin he noticed Harish Brown, the American CEO of Applogia walking down the corridor. His expression distant and clouded with fatigue. Harish wasn't just anyone; he was a self-made entrepreneur, a global thinker who rarely revealed much of himself. Rohil, with his keen instinct could see that the man was distracted. And Rohil was not one to overlook an opportunity.

Straightening his posture, he stood up and stepped out of the cabin. His face lighting up with an easy welcoming smile. Their eyes met.

"Good morning, Mr. Harish. How are you today?" Rohil began, his tone warm, deliberate, and full of charm.

Harish stopped, smirking faintly as he replied, *"Good morning, Rohil. Well, while my eyes are telling me it's daytime, my mind insists it's the middle of the night. Jet lag—crossing continents always seems to play games with the system."*

Rohil's mind worked quickly, recognizing the possibility to connect. He tilted his head slightly, concern mingling with admiration in his voice.

"That must be exhausting, sir. To be honest my team and I feel a bit jet-lagged ourselves—despite not moving an inch from our desks, let alone crossing continents. We've been losing track of time while pouring our energy into developing your personal favorite—the 'Savi Sports' app."

At that, Harish's eyes brightened, the exhaustion momentarily softening into approval. With a small smile, he said,

"That's fantastic, Rohil. Keep up the momentum—you're doing great job. As for me, I'll rely on coffee and the aroma of good coffee beans to wake my sleeping mind. They say nothing cures jet lag better

than the right flavours."

Harish had barely taken a step forward when Rohil's voice, smooth and assured, reached out like a hook on a fishing line.

"Sir, if you don't mind me asking—what's your favourite Indian cuisine?"

The question struck something deeper in Harish, stopping him in his tracks. The fatigue lifted from his face for a moment, replaced with a glint of nostalgia.

"No Punjabi," he said knowingly, *"can survive without butter chicken and a good tandoori. Me? I'm no exception."*
That was all Rohil needed to hear. He gestured subtly to Unni, who, as if reading his mind pulled up the online menu of the most renowned Punjabi restaurant in the town. Rohil invited Harish into the cabin, presenting the menu with an effortless charm. The tantalising visuals of vibrant curries and sizzling kebabs gleamed on the screen.

"Sir," Rohil said, his voice a perfect mix of persuasion and excitement, *"Lunch is on me. Let me take you to Punjabi's—they have the world's best butter chicken and tandoori. I promise you've never tasted anything like it."*

Harish studied the young man in front of him. Rohil had an energy about him, the kind that could elevate the dull grind of corporate life into something vibrant and full of purpose. Harish wasn't just impressed—he was intrigued. With a knowing smile, he quipped,

"You certainly know how to navigate things."

The compliment hung in the air like the promise of a good meal and Rohil basked in it. Knowing he had seized yet another moment to make an impression.

Rohil noticed the subtle shift in Harish's demeanour, the way his sharp eyes seemed to take stock of everything, even him. It was clear, Harish was testing him, perhaps probing to see whether Rohil's enthusiasm was mere surface-level charm to impress him or something deeper. But

Rohil wasn't one to falter. With an easy calm smile and unhurried tone, he redirected the conversation so smoothly it felt almost accidental and real like a thought that had just occurred to him.

"Sir," he began, his voice laced with subtle warmth, *"my grandmother always used to say the way to a man's heart is through his stomach. Give someone good food and happiness follows. It's basic, but it works. And a happy person doesn't even notice something like jet lag."*

Harish's gaze lingered on him for a beat and then to Rohil's slight surprise, Harish let out a deep, booming laugh—one so full and unrestrained that it seemed to shake off the fatigue that had clouded his face moments before. It was the kind of laughter that came from recognising a truth too simple to ignore.

"You might be onto something," Harish said between fits of laughter. *"Maybe all this restlessness I've been blaming on jet lag is just a craving—nothing more, nothing less. And if you can figure out what someone's craving for then you've already solved half the problem. For me, it's food. Butter chicken to be exact."* His smile widened as he clapped Rohil on the shoulder. *"Let's go for lunch, shall we?"*

In that moment, as Harish's energy seemed to lift, Rohil knew he had played his hand perfectly—neither too bold nor too safe. It hadn't been just about food or words after all. It had been about understanding what someone needed, even if they hadn't yet realized it themselves.

That afternoon at Punjabi's restaurant it wasn't just a casual lunch; it was a strategic moment and Rohil, always one step ahead wasn't going to let it slip by. He'd already prepared everything to perfection—Unni had pre-booked the table and pre-ordered dishes carefully tailored to Harish's tastes. The spread was exquisite and Harish, visibly impressed by the warm reception settled comfortably into the meal. The initial talk revolved around work but as the dishes kept coming and the mood lightened the conversation naturally shifted to leisurely topics. After dabbing his mouth with a napkin, Harish leaned back his sharp eyes glinting with curiosity, before asking,

"So, do you ski?"

The question caught Rohil off guard, his brow lifting in surprise.

"How did you know that, Sir?" he asked, intrigued.

Harish chuckled knowingly gesturing toward him. *"The photos in your cabin—they're not just decorative, are they? That one on the slope... you've got the stance of someone who knows exactly what they're doing."*

A grin spread across Rohil's face as he leaned back in his chair, a bit nostalgic himself. *"It's true. Sir, I always wanted to pursue adventure sports as a career but somehow, I ended up in this corporate world of technology."*

Harish grew quiet for a moment his expression softening, his thoughts clearly elsewhere. *"You 'wanted' to be a adventure sports professional,"* he said with a wistfulness that had nothing to do with their current setting. *"I 'was' into it. I was a skier. But then I got married and that part of my life was put on hold. From skier, I became... a husband,"* he said, *laughing lightly.*

Rohil laughed along with him and quickly quipped, *"That, Sir, is exactly why I've avoided getting married! No commitments, just free-flowing life."*

Harish chuckled but gave him a piece of advice, *"You're doing the right thing. Otherwise, those adventure photos on your cabin walls would have been replaced by family portraits by now."*

Unni, who was a keen observer of Rohil's uncanny ability to maneuver through conversations—and through corporate politics, butts in keeping himself in Harish's good graces, *"Sir,"* he said, flashing a cheeky grin, *"the two of you are so much alike."*

Aware of Unni's antics, Rohil cleared his throat and quickly redirected, *"Unni, why don't you order dessert?"*

Harish, still amused, chimed in. *"Unni, don't forget the rabri-jalebi*

(Indian Sweet)."

Rohil quickly added, as if to underline his attention to detail, *"Sir, rabri-jalebi was the first thing on the list!"*

As the meal continued Harish's curiosity circled back to Rohil's passion for skiing.

"So, where do you go skiing these days?" Harish asked.

Rohil's expression turned contemplative and he shrugged lightly.

"These days, it's rare—just when I manage to take a holiday. But whenever I get the chance, I head to the slopes in Solang Valley, Himachal. They're the best." As he spoke, Rohil noticed Harish growing quiet again, his focus seeming to drift somewhere far away. Sensing another opportunity to deepen the connection, Rohil leaned in just slightly his tone casual yet inviting.

"It's the right season for skiing now, Sir. Should we plan a trip to Himachal?"

Harish snapped back to the present and shook his head reluctantly. *"No, we can't. There's too much work right now,"* he said, though his hesitation gave him away.

Rohil, a master persuader knew exactly how to inch open that door. He smiled, shifting his pitch slightly. *"Sir, this year's office trip is still pending. If you approve, we could plan something around that. Say the word—I'll handle all the details."* His tone was light almost playful but the way he slipped logic into his suggestion made it near impossible to refuse.

Harish leaned back in his chair, still debating. *"Really…"* he murmured, his indecision hanging in the air. Rohil recognized the moment—the brief crack in Harish's resolve—and leaned into it just enough, knowing exactly when to push and when to let a little silence do the work. For Rohil, every pause, every flicker of hesitation was an opening—and he never let one pass without making his move.

Rohil bent slightly across the table, his tone calm yet filled with conviction. *"Sir, everything for this office trip is already in place. We've partnered with trip organizers who handle all the logistics. All we need is Mr. Gautam's approval and we're off to Solang Valley."*

Harish, still mulling over the idea, tapped his fingers lightly on the table. *"Alright,"* he said after a pause, his tone noncommittal. *"Run it by Mr. Gautam. If he agrees go ahead but there's no pressure from my side."*

Rohil smiled, a quiet confidence glimmering in his eyes. He knew he could pull this off—not just as a simple office outing but as a perfect opportunity to strengthen bonds within the team and more importantly, build better rapport with Harish.

After treating Harish to his favorite lunch—a clever ploy to satisfy not just his craving for food but also his deeper hunger for attention and respect—Rohil secured a unique, albeit fragile foothold in Harish's mind. Recognizing the need to solidify this connection, Rohil delved into meticulous research, uncovering every thread of Harish's journey—from his childhood quirks to his ascent as CEO of App-Logia. Armed with this well-woven tapestry of insights, Rohil prepared for his next calculated move to fortify their burgeoning rapport.

As evening settled over the office, Harish and Gautam walked through the quiet corridor, their conversation flowing easily—until a sudden flicker in the lights was followed by complete darkness. The power had gone out, plunging everything into an eerie silence. They hesitated, then carefully navigated their way, their hands brushing against the walls for guidance. As they turned a corner towards the office floor, a soft, golden glow broke through the darkness. There, in the center of the room stood a cake with flickering candles. Before they could react the electricity surged back to life revealing a sea of smiling faces.

"Happy Birthday, Mr. Harish!" the entire office erupted in cheers. A wave of laughter rippled through the crowd as Harish's gaze fell upon the cake—his name had been amusingly misspelled as "Hash

Brown." Chuckling, he shook his head and leaned forward to cut the cake, only for the office to explode into an unexpected spectacle.

The moment the first slice was made, Rohil's team sprang into action, seamlessly launching into a choreographed Bollywood dance routine. The energy was infectious, the floor alive with synchronized movements, cheers, and clapping.

Before Harish could fully absorb the moment, Mysha grabbed his hand and pulled him into the dance, his initial surprise giving way to reluctant amusement. On the other side of the room, Abeer's team clapped along, showing their enthusiasm though none of them had joined the performance—except for Amit, who was already moving in sync with Rohil's team.

Abeer lingered in the shadows watching with an expression that suggested he had no intention of joining. But Mysha, insistent as ever had other ideas. With a playful smirk she caught his arm and yanked him into the center of the crowd. At first, Abeer moved stiffly, unwilling but the moment his body found the rhythm, something shifted. His hesitant steps transformed into confident, fluid movements—he was an incredible dancer. For a moment all eyes were on him, admiration flashing across faces. Yet, just as quickly as he had allowed himself to indulge in the celebration, he slipped away retreating to his quiet corner.

The evening flowed into a grand feast, a testament to Rohil's meticulous planning. Every detail had been thought through, and it was clear he had left no stone unturned to make the night special for Harish. His efforts did not go unnoticed. As the celebration wound down, Harish, now a little tipsy, a little sentimental pulled Rohil into an embrace.

"Thank you, Rohil," he murmured, his voice carrying the weight of nostalgia. *"You remind me of my younger, livelier days. Don't let life's burdens crush this side of you. Keep your spirits high—and keep lifting the spirit of this office too."*

A satisfied smile played on Rohil's lips. He had orchestrated every move with precision, weaving himself seamlessly into his boss Harish's good graces. The art of proximity, the dance of influence—he had mastered it all. And now he stood victorious, knowing he had secured his place where it truly mattered.

RIVALS IN THE SNOW

Abeer sat in his cabin, absentmindedly polishing his skis, the rhythmic motion almost meditative. The soft gleam of the polished wood reflected his thoughts—distant, untouched, like a past he no longer reached for. The door swung open breaking his moment of stillness. Rohil stepped in, an easy smirk playing on his lips.

"You really had us all fooled," he said, arms crossed as he leaned against the doorframe. *"That was some performance at the party. Who knew you had moves like that?"*

Abeer didn't look up. *"Thanks."* His voice was neutral, offering nothing more than necessary.

There was always an undercurrent between them—sharp, electric, charged with unspoken rivalry. Rohil thrived on it constantly seeking an edge, while Abeer remained indifferent engaging only when provoked.

"So," Rohil continued, his tone laced with casual mockery, *"trading in Ski boots for dancing shoes? Amit mentioned you're not coming for the ski trip."*

Abeer's grip on the cloth tightened slightly before he set it down. He had no desire to entertain this conversation but courtesy dictated a response. *"There's no point walking a path that leads nowhere."* His words were simple although the weight behind them was unmistakable.

Rohil, of course couldn't resist. *"You know, skis don't shine from polish. They shine from cutting through snow. Maybe you should actually use them sometime."*

Abeer smirked, unfazed. He knew Rohil well—always pushing, always testing. *"Things done with the mind have reason. Things done with the heart—those are often without one. My connection with these skis doesn't go beyond this cabin anymore."* Abeer declared with a sense of finality.

Their conversations were never just words. They were unspoken duels layered with meaning, their competitive spirit woven into every exchange.

"You know, Abeer," Rohil said, eyes glinting with mischief, *"I think I like you more than I like my girlfriend."*

Abeer finally looked up, smirking. *"Mysha won't be thrilled to hear that confession."*

Rohil shrugged, unbothered. *"You keep me on my toes. Push me beyond my limits. Sometimes, even I'm surprised at what I can do because of you. You challenge me, bro."*

Abeer's expression didn't change. *"Good for you."*

Rohil leaned in slightly, as if he is whispering some eternal truth. *"I watch your every move. Stay one step ahead. Because, my friend, I don't like to lose."*

Abeer set his skis aside, his next words slow and deliberate, cutting through Rohil's bravado like a blade. *"That's why I don't see you as a real player. You play just to beat me. I play to set a new benchmark for myself. To chase the feeling that comes with conquering a challenge. I don't care who's on the other side."*

The words landed but Rohil wasn't one to retreat. He pushed forward. *"You probably don't remember but that inter-college climbing competition you won? That was my game. I was supposed to compete. Just didn't get the chance."*

Abeer let out a soft laugh, the kind that held no warmth. *"How long are you going to grieve that loss? Even if you had competed, you wouldn't have won. You need me to feed your ego, Rohil. But to me—you don't even exist."*

For the first time, Rohil's smirk faltered but it returned just as quickly. He took a breath, masking whatever flicker of emotion had surfaced. *"Fine. Don't come skiing. Just admit I'm the sharpest guy around"*

Abeer stood, buttoning his coat, taking his time before stepping closer, his gaze unwavering. *"Alright, if it's about that, then I'll come. Someone has to knock some sense into you."*

Just as the tension thickened, Abeer's phone buzzed. He glanced at it, answering with effortless ease. *"Excuse me."* And with that he walked out, leaving Rohil standing there, forced to swallow the last word he had hoped to claim. Rohil clenched his jaw but his practiced smile remained. The game wasn't over. Not yet.

The entire office had gathered at the ski resort in Solang Valley, their energy high with adrenaline as they embraced the thrill of skiing. Laughter echoed through the snowy slopes as beginners like Unni, Komal, and Mysha took their first wobbly steps on skis—some tumbling, some gliding for a few meters before gravity had its way.

Amidst the cheerful chaos on the professional Giant Slalom track, the organizers had set up a competition. The boss, Harish had the privilege of inaugurating the event, and the spark in his eyes was unmistakable—it was as if he had found a long-lost childhood toy. Catching Rohil's gaze, he silently thanked him for reconnecting him with a passion buried under years of corporate routine.

Dressed in full gear, Harish launched himself down the track. His technique, though rusty, carried the grace of someone who once owned the slopes. Minor slips marked his run, but for someone who hadn't skied in over a decade, he did remarkably well, drawing cheers and applause as he completed the circuit in 1 minute and 30 seconds. The crowd's excitement surged as Rohil prepared for his turn. Ever the showman, he twirled his ski poles like a juggler, walking toward the start line with an air of absolute confidence. His aggressive stance sent a wave of expectation through the spectators—his team especially holding their breath, certain he would dominate the track.

As the whistle blew, Rohil descended his maneuvers breathtaking and his turns razor-sharp. He sliced through the course with skill never seen before, reaching the finish line in just 1 minute and 28 seconds. The crowd erupted in awe.

Even Unni, ever the skeptic, turned to Mysha and admitted his surprise, *"I thought Rohil was all talk. But damn, he can ski."*

Mysha, who knew Rohil all too well, smirked knowingly, *"That's his charm. He talks big but he makes sure to back it up."*

The organizer took the microphone, his voice ringing through the valley. *"Guys, give it up for Mr. Rohil! 1 minute and 28 seconds—the best timing on this slope so far!"*

Rohil basked in the glory, his excitement barely concealed as he approached Abeer, his expression laced with subtle arrogance. With a sly smile he shook Abeer's hand. *"All the best, bro."* He wishes, more out of arrogance for clocking the best timing than out of genuine goodwill.

Abeer, however, remained as composed as ever. Unlike Rohil's flamboyant energy his presence was calm and assured, radiating a quiet confidence that was neither intimidating nor boastful but rather inviting. As he walked towards the start line, the crowd—despite his elusive nature in the office—found themselves drawn to him, cheering for him as if compelled by an invisible force. Even without personal connections, his sincerity and humility made people want to support him. The only one displeased with this shift in energy was Rohil, whose excitement dimmed ever so slightly.

Abeer closed his eyes for a moment at the starting line, exhaling deeply before fixing his gaze on the track. As the whistle blew, he surged forward. His technique was flawless—his turns fluid, his balance impeccable. Unlike Rohil's aggressive style, Abeer moved with effortless elegance, every motion precise and efficient. The snowflakes swirled behind him creating a white dust storm as he cut through the track, finishing at an astonishing 1 minute and 25 seconds. The organizer didn't hesitate before declaring Abeer the undisputed winner.

The moment hit Rohil like a blow. Just moments ago victory had seemed certain, yet here he was, bested in front of the entire office. He struggled to accept the loss. His mind spiraled into suspicion—was there a mistake? A miscalculation? Even a harmless smile from the organizer felt like mockery. *"I think there's been an error in the timing,"* he objected to organizer, his frustration barely masked.

The organizer unfazed held up the stopwatch. *"Sir, we organize professional competitions. There's no room for mistakes. See for yourself—the time is still displayed: 1 minute and 25 seconds."*

Rohil's eyes darkened, though he maintained an outward calm. *"Maybe you stopped the watch before Abeer reached the finish line,"* he accused organizer subtly.

The organizer scoffed. *"Are you serious? Do you think Abeer is my friend that I'd rig the results? You're being ridiculous."*

Harish, having observed the exchange, sensed the need for intervention before things escalated. *"Rohil, Abeer is the true winner. I've never seen a performance like that,"* he stated firmly.

Rohil's frustration spiked at Harish's words. *"Sir, I can't lose! There must have been some mistake."*

Harish, ever the logical entrepreneur decided to settle it with facts. He asked for the competition footage and played both Rohil's and Abeer's runs in slow motion, analyzing each move. *"Rohil, your turns are sharp but you twist your body too abruptly at each turning pole. Because of that you can't bend fully and the friction from the snow slows you down."*

He then switched to Abeer's footage. *"See how Abeer anticipates the turn before reaching the pole? His body nearly brushes the snow, keeping his turning radius longer and angle lower. This reduces friction and keeps his speed consistent."*

Harish's analysis was irrefutable, leaving no room for doubt. Rohil walked away, his pride wounded, his mind burning with determination. Losing wasn't an option. If he couldn't win now, he would train until he could.

As the night deepened and the valley turned frigid, Rohil remained on the track ruthlessly practicing his turns. Mysha stayed by his side keeping time with the stopwatch, encouraging him through each failed attempt. He skied with obsessive dedication, stopping only to check his lap times. He refused to rest. The harsh wind bit at his face, exhaustion clawed at his body but he pushed through. And then, as the first rays of morning light touched the slopes, he finally did it.

Mysha gasped, exhilarated. *"1:24:50! You did it, Rohil!"* She threw her arms around him sharing his triumph.

Rohil sprinted to Abeer's tent, shaking him awake. Groggy, Abeer stepped outside rubbing his eyes as Rohil shoved the stopwatch in his face. For a moment, Abeer stared at it in disbelief before throwing his hands in the air and laughing. As he turned to retreat into his tent, he looked back with a smirk. *"Congratulations, Rohil. At least you let poor Mysha rest—she had a long day yesterday."*

His tone was nonchalant as if none of it really mattered. To Abeer, victory wasn't a pedestal nor was defeat a wound. But for Rohil, it was everything. Winning wasn't just about being the best—it was about proving himself, upholding his pride, maintaining his image as the one who always comes out on top no matter the cost.

And though Abeer turned away, one thing lingered in his mind—Rohil's unrelentingly determination. His obsession with winning even at the expense of rules, limits, and fairness. He wasn't sure if that was admirable or dangerous. Perhaps it was both.

BREAKING THE CODE

Late at night the conference hall of 'App-Logia' was still lit up, the large projector screen displaying the final prototype of the highly anticipated "Savi Sports" app. Abeer's and Rohil's teams had been working persistently for months, perfecting every detail before the big presentation. As the clock struck midnight, most of the team had left but Amit remained, meticulously running through the final UX checks. His eyes bloodshot from endless hours in front of the screen. He scanned every menu, every detail with pin point accuracy. The weight of tomorrow's presentation loomed over them all—approval from the top executives would mean the project could move forward, boosting the entire team's morale; while rejection would be a devastating setback to delivery timeline, jeopardizing both their reputations and the company's standing in the industry.

Usually composed, Abeer was inwardly anxious today as he stepped into the hall.

"Amit, it's past midnight. Tomorrow is a big day. Go home and get some rest." Abeer advised.

Amit, barely blinking, replied, *"Just one final check, then we are done."*

Abeer took a deep breath, surveying their work. *"I think we've built exactly what we set out to achieve."*

Amit smiled. *"Right, sir."*

"Good night and all the best," Abeer said with a warm smile before turning to leave.

"Good night, sir." Amit said with a polite nod.

After completing the final checks, Amit packed up for the day, and just as he was leaving, Unni stepped into the hall. *"Leave the system on,"* he requested. *"I need to run some last-minute UI checks."*

Amit, too exhausted to question it, vacated his seat. As soon as he left, Unni plugged an external drive into the system navigating directly into the app's JavaScript framework. His fingers moved rapidly across the keyboard as he inserted new lines of code into the front-end interface.

By morning, the conference hall was transformed into a stage for the grand presentation. A massive screen loomed behind the podium, mirroring every move on the app. The entire office had gathered, the atmosphere buzzing with anticipation, reminiscent of a high-profile tech launch event. Rohil and Abeer stood ready, each about to showcase their team's work. Tension was thick in the air—this was the culmination of their hard-work, a defining moment for both teams.

Rohil took the stage first. Despite being a confident leader, the pressure was getting to him. To break the tension, he decided to start with a light comment. *"Wow, the whole office is here. Seems like no one has any actual work to do!"*Laughter rippled through the room.

Harish, seated in the front row, smirked. *"A pressure cooker only whistles when there's enough steam. But whether the food inside is perfectly cooked or completely burnt—we won't know until we lift the lid. So, Mr. Rohil, it's time to reveal what you've got for us."*

Gautam grinned. *"Ah, but if the rubber seal is faulty, sometimes the air escapes from underneath, and the food never cooks at all."*

Another wave of laughter spread through the audience, lightening the atmosphere. Gautam, keeping an eye on the clock, interjected again, *"Let's see if your whistle blows or if all the air just leaks out. Start already!"* Both Harish and Gautam's comments suggest that bosses rise to the top because of their intelligence and wit.

Rohil launched into his pitch, his tone turning serious. *"Harish sir, what's your favorite dessert in the summer season?"*

Harish, intrigued, replied, *"Ice cream."*

"And why do you love ice cream in the summers?" Rohil asked next.

"There's nothing better than enjoying a cold, creamy ice cream on a scorching hot day."

Rohil nodded. *"That 'feel good' factor is what we want to create every time a customer opens our app. We aim to evoke emotion. In summer, our interface will feature cool refreshing hues and breezy fonts; in winter, it will shift to warm, cozy tones."*

As he spoke, the projector displayed sleek UI mockups—icy blues and crisp whites for summer, deep ambers and soft reds for winter. The audience was captivated. Harish's eyes lit up. *"That's brilliant! Imagine using India's summers to promote mountains and hill stations by encouraging sports like skiing and mountaineering—and winter to promote Goa's beaches and water activities like surfing and rafting. Ingenious idea, Rohil!"*

Emboldened by the response, Rohil added, *"And to enhance this, we'll feature immersive visuals—snow-capped peaks, shimmering beaches— drawing users into the experience."*

Applause filled the hall. Gautam checked his watch. *"Rohil, this is impressive. Anything else to add?"*

With confidence, Rohil declared, *"Our goal is simple—once a customer clicks on our app, they shouldn't leave without making a purchase."*

On that note he exited the stage to thunderous applause, clearly having left an impression.

Now, it was Abeer's turn. He stepped up right away and, coincidentally, began with a question: "What's the hardest thing to get from a customer?"

A collective response echoed through the hall. *"Money."*

Abeer shook his head. *"Wrong. The hardest thing is their time. If a customer takes time to explore our app, they're already invested. Our goal is to make every moment spent on our app worthwhile, ensuring users leave feeling happy, satisfied, and never regretting their time with us. And that's where our interface comes in—simple, intuitive, seamless."*

Abeer exchanged a glance with Harish, watching for any hint of a reaction. Intrigued Harish leaned forward, his eyes narrowing with curiosity. *"Go on,"* he urged.

"Sir, India has the infrastructure for adventure sports, yet demand remains low. We will handle everything—locations, gear, trainers, bookings. But where will we find the adventure enthusiasts and most importantly how?"

Gautam, eager to hear more, prompted, *"Get to the point Abeer."*

Abeer smirked. *"The answer is a multilingual app. India is a land of incredible diversity with at least 22 officially recognized languages spoken across its regions. To truly connect with this vast market, we must tailor our approach to resonate with each linguistic and cultural landscape. Therefore from day one, our app will speak to users in their native language, creating an immediate connection."*

A hushed admiration filled the room. Abeer's words carried weight—not because he was loud, but because they were precise. Abeer's presentation had a clear edge over Rohil's, further fueling their professional rivalry between them. He moved to the final demonstration.

The screen displayed a warm welcome: *"Hello/Namaste."* The IVR played, greeting users in different regional languages.

"If you're in Punjab, the app will greet you in Punjabi. In Maharashtra, Marathi."

As Abeer demonstrated the drop-down menu for activities, accommodations, and equipment; he clicked on the clothing section to showcase how it would direct users to relevant sports gear store of 'Savi Sports'.

The screen changed. Instead of displaying a professional 'Savi sportswear store', it showcased a lingerie store with scantily clad models.

The room went silent. Abeer, taken aback, quickly clicked on another section—equipment. The same lingerie store popped up. He frantically navigated through the app but every link led to the same embarrassing page.

A murmur spread through the hall. Faces turned toward each other in confusion. Abeer, horrified, stepped back. His throat went dry.

Without another word, he stepped off the stage, his confidence shattered. A moment ago, he had commanded the room. Now, he could barely look up. Humiliated, he walked out of the conference hall, leaving behind an eerie silence.

TRANSMUTATION

Abeer sat alone in his office late into the night, his fingers absentmindedly dipping into a jar of climbing chalk resting on the side table. The fine white powder, designed to enhance grip and absorb moisture became a strange source of solace. He rubbed it between his palms as if by coating his hands he could shield himself from the sting of the humiliation he had suffered on the podium.

The human spirit is a dynamic force—constantly shifting, evolving, and adapting—and Abeer was no different. The shame he had endured twisted into helplessness, then frustration. He grappled with the realization that he had no control over what had transpired. It felt like he was being pulled into a black hole, sinking into despair. But despair soon burned into rage. His eyes now bloodshot flared with unrestrained anger. Without hesitation he grabbed his climbing gear, tossed it into his SUV, and drove away into the night.

The mountain stood before him, the same one he and his father used to climb together. Recklessly, almost feverishly, Abeer ascended its unforgiving face. He climbed not for glory or conquest but to rid himself of the overwhelming surge of pain threatening to consume him. Every jagged rock tore into his skin, bruising and battering him but he pressed on, undeterred. His breath came in ragged bursts, his body screamed in protest, but he reached the peak—bloodied, exhausted, and transformed. With trembling hands he pulled out a piece of paper and a pen, his crimson-stained fingers leaving smudges on the pristine sheet as he began to write.

Hours later, just before dawn, he stepped quietly into his mother's bedroom and placed the letter beside her pillow.

The first rays of morning light streamed through the windows as Abeer sat across from his mother at the dining table, eating breakfast in silence. Sunita, his mother, unfolded the letter and read it with a long, deep sigh. A faint, knowing smile crossed her lips as she placed it on the table and spoke, almost to herself.

"The Frozen Himalayan Competition," she murmured, pausing before shaking her head. *"It's in your DNA."*

She picked up the letter once more and waved it at Abeer. *"I expected this a long time ago."*

Abeer looked up, startled, before snatching the letter from her hands. *"Mom, this is all because of you! How could you have expected this?"*

Sunita met his gaze calmly. *"I think you should listen to your heart. No one should force their children into a life they don't choose."*

Abeer stopped eating mid-bite, his mind reeling. *"What? You're suddenly doing a complete 180 degree turn? What am I supposed to make of this?"*

His mother's expression softened as she confessed, *"I was afraid you'd become like Veer Singh (referring to his father) a failed person. That insecurity haunted me. I always wanted a stable and secure career for you. But now, I know you have a backup plan."*

Abeer studied her, the emotions still raw in his voice. *"And what if I never want to come back and completely abandon all your so called backup plans?"*

Sunita smirked. *"You're old and responsible enough to understand and prioritize your goals in life."*

Something shifted in Abeer. The invisible weight he had carried for so long—of duty, of expectation—felt lighter. For years, he had shaped his life to fit his mother's dreams, silencing his own. But as clarity settled within him he realized the burden of obligation had finally lifted. For the first time, he dared to dream for himself.

His mother's wisdom lay not in controlling him anymore, but in guiding him, in letting him find his own path. As Abeer rose from the table, Sunita reached out, her voice filled with both love and fear.

"Take care of yourself out there Abeer. These mountains… they have a way of taking things from us."

Abeer hesitated for just a moment before stepping forward and embracing her. Sunita's eyes glistened with unshed tears.

"I'm sorry, Abeer, for putting you through all of this."

Abeer held her tightly, knowing that no words were needed. In that quiet moment, they both understood—this was not an ending, but a beginning.

FROM PAYCHECKS TO PEAKS

The office buzzed with energy as Rohil went from desk to desk, handing out chocolates to his colleagues to celebrate the accolades he received for his presentation. He spotted Abeer walking by, he called out to him and extended a chocolate with a smile.

"These are my absolute favorite," he said warmly.

Abeer, however, was still simmering inside, haunted by what had transpired during the presentation. He kept his face expressionless but accepted the chocolate with a silent nod. Looking at it with disdain, he unwrapped it and ate it anyway, his movements stiff with restrained anger. Then, with a firm handshake and a sharp gaze he muttered,

"Congratulations, you con artist."

Rohil, perceptive as ever immediately picked up on Abeer's hostility. His smirk widened as he met Abeer's aggression with equal intensity. Rohil sweeps his gaze across the office floor, his voice rising to capture everyone's attention.

"Keep that applause coming, folks—every round of praise just gets sweeter. Don't hold back; I'm soaking up the spotlight!" he quipped. Though Rohil spoke to the entire office, his words had a sharp edge, unmistakably directed at Abeer. Beneath his excitement lingered the sting of his defeat on the ski slopes during the office trip—a loss he hadn't forgotten.

Abeer turned toward the office window, taking a deep breath, attempting to suppress the fury building within him. *"You're getting a promotion, right?"* he said in a measured tone. *"Take it lightly, man. Otherwise, you'll crumble under the weight of your own arrogance."*

Rohil scoffed. *"For your information, bro, this isn't arrogance. It's called confidence."*

That was the last straw for Abeer. His voice rose, his restraint breaking. *"No. This is swindling, Rohil."*

Abeer's this sudden outburst sent ripples across the office floor. Heads popped up from cubicles, eyes locked onto the unfolding confrontation. But neither Abeer nor Rohil wavered under the unwarranted attention.

Rohil's expression darkened as he fired back. *"I admit, your UX interface was robust. But if it keeps redirecting users to lingerie stores, it only reveals your perverted mindset."* Adding a sly smile to seal his remark.

Abeer's jaw tightened. He knew exactly what had happened the night before the presentation. He didn't need to mince his words. His accusation was laced with bitter truth.

"That day the system would have worked flawlessly if Unni didn't exploit unscrupulous codes to breach actual commands and the codes hadn't redirected it to a lingerie store over and over again. But I see now—you guys just have a thing for lingerie shopping." Abeer said, sneering, his voice dripping with mockery.

Rohil smirked, unfazed. *"Mr. Abeer, you're throwing around baseless allegations. I challenge you to prove them."*

But Abeer didn't care for validation. He knew what mattered to him. *"I don't make it a habit to whine over what's lost,"* he said, his voice steady. Then, with a firm nod, he declared, *"You got one thing right, Rohil. In this office"*—he swept his hand around—*"I can't beat you."*

Rohil seized the moment to twist the knife. *"Well, at least you've realized it, even if a little late."*

Abeer clenched his fists. The idea of inserting malicious codes to sabotage someone's work was an act of a petty, insecure mind. He wasn't about to let Rohil walk away without knowing exactly what he thought of him. *"You don't play your moves based on talent. You play on deceit and manipulation,"* he spat.

Rohil chuckled, patting Abeer's shoulder mockingly. *"Come on, Abeer, it's all professional. No hard feelings, bro."*

Abeer brushed off Rohil's hand with a swift jerk, as if flicking away a speck of dust, a smirk curling at the edges of his lips. His voice was cool, edged with an almost playful disdain.

"The real problem isn't that people bend the rules under the guise of professionalism," he said, his gaze unwavering. *"The problem is that everyone sees it as smartness, not dishonesty. And in the end, everything gets justified."*

But Rohil wasn't one to shrink under scrutiny. He thrived on opposition, relishing the chance to turn it into a game of words and wit.

"It's simple, Abeer," he shot back, his tone laced with amused condescension. *"The one who seizes an opportunity is the one who truly deserves it. You're a sportsman—show some sportsmanship. Accept your defeat and next time give it your all. Always stay positive."*

Abeer had heard enough. He wasn't the kind to accept shallow logic wrapped in fancy words. His smirk deepened, his eyes burning with something far sharper than mere disagreement.

"A true player doesn't prove his worth in boardrooms, Rohil. He proves it thousands of feet above, where the mountains are merciless. Up there, it's just you and the peaks—no deceit, no shortcuts, just trust. The mountains don't care about opportunists. They can take lives in minutes, without warning. But if you show courage and talent, even Mount Everest will bow to your determination. Because up there, it's not about ego—it's about mutual respect."

Rohil let out a mocking laugh, shaking his head as if Abeer had just recited some foolish fable. *"You sure talk a good game. But all this so-called wisdom of yours? It doesn't hold up in reality. That long-winded speech you just gave was utter nonsense."*

Abeer merely smirked, knowing full well the weight of his words. And to prove his point, he threw down a challenge right then and there, in the heart of the corporate world.

"If you ever want to see a real winner, come to 'The Frozen Himalayan Competition.' In minutes, I'll shatter your confidence—and then, you'll understand exactly what my words meant."

With that, he nudged Rohil lightly with his shoulder, turning on his heel with the quiet confidence of a man who had already made his decision. He walked away, leaving behind an air of finality.

Rohil slid his hands into his pockets, smirking with equal arrogance.

"I don't lose, Mr. Abeer," he murmured under his breath. *"I take victory, no matter what."*

That moment changed everything. Abeer handed in his resignation the very next day. The office walls had never been his battlefield, nor had suits and sprints ever been his armor. The mountains had always called out to him, and now, finally he was listening.

This was more than a decision—it was a homecoming. A return to the dream he had once sketched in his childhood, now bursting into reality with limitless possibilities and an unbreakable determination. The corporate world would forget him soon enough. But the mountains? They were waiting.

CHAPTER – 3

TETHERED BY FATE

At the Indian Climbing Institute (ICI) in Manali, Neet stood before her class, a detailed map of the rock projected on the screen. The lengths and dimensions of the upcoming climbing route were meticulously marked. Unbeknownst to her, Abeer sat quietly at the back his eyes fixed on her, captivated by her radiant presence. Neet addressed the class, instructing them to start climbing from the north face and study the rock thoroughly before scaling it. *"No student will share equipment,"* she warned, recalling past incidents. *"Mountaineering is a serious and dangerous sport. Make your own checklist and double-check it. We meet tomorrow at 7 a.m. at the rock."* Eager with anticipation, the students hung onto Neet's every word, absorbing her advice with keen attention and genuine enthusiasm.

The next morning, at the base of the towering mountain, Neet and her students gathered, the crisp air buzzing with excitement. From afar, Abeer observed Neet, her presence as vibrant as the morning sun. As she prepared to lead the climb, she instructed student,

"I'll lead. A climber and their partner share a bond as deep as that of a husband and wife—one mistake can cost both their lives. And here, the entire class is tied to the same rope. Imagine how many 'partners' will go down together with just one small misstep. So, be cautious."

A dash of humor in Neet's instructions lit up the faces of the attentive students with cheerful smiles. Neet began her ascent, her students following.

From below, Abeer watched the line of students ascending, their silhouettes tracing the skyward path with determination. suddenly he sprang into action to climb, choosing a different route. His shadow, swift and fluid against the sun caught Neet's attention. His grip was firm, his climb effortless, more a sprint than a struggle. Intrigued, Neet hastened her pace her composure cracking, as though someone had suddenly slammed a foot on a car's accelerator. Swift as a mountain breeze weaving through the pines, Neet reached the summit—but not before securing the ropes for the students climbing behind her.

Reaching the peak ahead of her class Neet scanned for the mysterious climber. Unexpectedly the flutter of a jacket caught her attention—a lone figure stood at the edge of the rock with his back towards her. As Neet approached, she spoke with a knowing edge, as though she had unraveled the person's identity by reading nothing more than his shadow. Neet remarked,

"The way you grip the rock—it's hard to tell where you end and the mountain begins. I can recognize you by your climbing stance. That's why I always enjoy watching you climb."

Abeer turned, his voice tinged with mock complaint, *"You're quite the friend you left me to rot in the corporate world."*

"I tried," Neet retorted, *"but you're stubborn. You wouldn't buzz, so I left you to your own devices. I don't like forcing people."*

Abeer bristled at her blunt honesty. *"That's what you call trying? You should've pushed me to do what I'm meant for—no one knows me better than you. So much for 'a friend in need is a friend indeed.'"*

Neet's defenses softened, emotion seeping through her words. *"I see friendship differently. A true friend lets you make your own choices and simply waits for you to come around."*

Abeer's brows lifted, probing further, *"So… you were actually waiting for me?"*

Neet, ever guarded, cloaked her feelings in wisdom. *"Talent and passion make a dangerous mix, Abeer. You can't stop it; you can only wait for the right time. And the right time… well, that takes time to come by."*

Abeer, testing the waters of their long-lost connection, questioned, *"And what if that moment had never arrived? What if I had never returned?"*

Neet paused, reflecting on their journey so far, was it lingering nostalgia or something deeper? She answered, her voice philosophical,

"Whatever was destined for our relationship would have happened. But that would have been a true loss for the climbing as a sport. After all, it's the only sport where your opponent is 4.5 billion years old. No rival is more ruthless than nature. That's why every summit conquered sparks hope—and humanity has thrived on hope for millennia."

Abeer sensed her shift, steering the conversation towards deeper nuances, Abeer poses a question. *"So, what difference does it make whether I climb or not?"*

Neet's eyes sparkled with conviction. *"A single genius can change the world's perspective. Climbing isn't even considered a sport in our country—it needs a player like you. To show people that true sports aren't just between two teams but between you and yourself."* Neet's passion for climbing stands at the forefront—she is more than a teacher or a guide; she is a visionary, determined to propel the sport to new heights. But to make that dream a reality, she needs a climber like Abeer, someone who can inspire and draw others to the sport. The bond between a sport and its athlete is symbiotic—they elevate each other, reaching their true potential together.

Completely captivated by Neet's perspective Abeer expressed his appreciation with a playful touch of humor, *"From now on, you're the*

G.O.A.T. (Greatest of All Time) of climbing. If cricket players heard your lecture, they'd trade their bats for ropes."

Neet chuckled, a hint of embarrassment flickering through her smile at having unveiled her passion for climbing. *"What can I say? Giving orientation speeches has become second nature to me. Add a dash of philosophy, stir the hunger for adventure and thrill—and watch the students line up to enroll from my climbing classes."*

Their playful banter rekindled the warmth of their past. Abeer grinned, *"So, this is how you fool innocent students!"*

Neet shot back with a cackle, *"Not fool—motivate. After all, I need new climbers every year to keep my salary running."*

Abeer's eyes glinted with mischief. *"Well, you've got one now—will you train me?"*

In answer, Neet pulled him into a warm hug, nodding with a smile.

They walked away, hand in hand descending the mountain. Their bond reforged in the timeless duel between mind and heart—where the mind clings to the material world, and the heart follows the call of dreams and love.

STALLED HEARTS

Rohil's life was a hard-nosed corporate climb—fast, sharp, and utterly consuming. As an executive director at App-Logia, he was scaling the corporate ladder with a hunger that never seemed to fade. Every victory only sharpened his ambition and now his sights were set on the firm's top position, CTO. A title he would claim by carefully outmaneuvering his boss, Gautam. But while his career had a clear trajectory, his personal life was a different story—one he barely understood. Love, relationships, marriage? They felt like abstract concepts and unnecessary distractions from his bigger goals.

The winding road led them to the edge of a cliff, where the mountains stretched endlessly into the horizon. Rohil's brand-new SUV came to a smooth halt and he stepped out with Mysha by his side. The air was crisp, tinged with the scent of trees but there was a silence between them; heavier than the looming sky above.

A boy from the roadside café approached with a menu but Rohil didn't need to look.

"One 'bund makkhan (buttered bun)', a plate of paneer pakoras (Indian cottage cheese fritters), noodles, and two masala chai (Tea)," he ordered effortlessly before turning to Mysha. *"Anything else?"*

She barely lifted her gaze. Her voice was distant, her thoughts elsewhere.

He had noticed it for a while now—the quiet storm brewing inside her, the way her smile had dulled, the way her words were fewer, heavier.

That was why he had brought her here, hoping to break the silent discontent that had wrapped itself around them like an invisible fog. He tried to coax her back with his usual charm.

"Go on, order whatever you love to snack on. After all, enjoying the food you love brings a sense of contentment—and a soul filled with contentment is a truly happy one."

Mysha's face hardened. *"Stop it, Rohil,"* she snapped, her eyes blazing. *"Love isn't just a word to be thrown around—it holds a depth you can't even begin to grasp. Coming from you it feels hollow, stripping it of the sanctity it deserves."* And just like that, the playful moment crafted by Rohil shattered.

Mysha turned and walked towards the edge, staring out at the vast nothingness. Rohil watched her, exhaling. He had always been a man of strategy, of careful maneuvering. Direct confrontations weren't his style—he preferred to talk his way through things, to twist conversations until they landed exactly where he wanted.

Mysha was different—too tender for a world that preyed on emotions. In love, nothing stung deeper than emotional blackmail, and with Rohil, she bore its weight in silence. Her gaze stretched toward the horizon, seeking solace in the distant peaks, whispering her unspoken thoughts to the mountains and the endless sky beyond,

"People like you, Rohil who preach about love, often fail to understand its true nature. Love is elusive, a complex emotion that defies simple definition. It molds itself to the needs and desires of each individual, existing in a form unique to them alone. It takes countless shapes—your love may look nothing like mine, yet it remains love all the same. So don't cling to the word itself; seek to understand its essence instead. It should always be seen from the perspective of the one who loves."

That did it. The dam finally broke. She turned to Rohil who was standing behind, *"From your perspective, it doesn't resemble love at all. It looks like a slow, inevitable betrayal unraveling before my eyes."* Mysha said, her voice sharp, cutting through the cold air.

Rohil's lips curled into a small knowing smile. He had led them right to the core of their conflict. Master of deception, Rohil, rather than allowing words to hang in the air, bridged the distance between them. His lips capturing hers in a kiss that spoke louder and truer than any conversation ever could. For a moment, Mysha gave in—her body melting into his, her breath catching. But then, just as suddenly, she pulled away. Her eyes sharp and unyielding, locked onto his.

"Will you marry me, Rohil?" Mysha spoke with unwavering clarity, her words flowing from the depths of her whole being.

There it was. The question he had known would come, the one he had dreaded. He let out a quiet laugh, shaking his head.

"We're too young, Mysha. And anyway, marriage ruins romance. Let's not spoil this. Let's just… enjoy it while it lasts."

Mysha's jaw tightened. *"I'm not asking you to marry me tomorrow, Rohil,"* she said, her voice steady. *"I need to know where we stand—how you truly feel and what your intentions are regarding marriage. Being left in this state of uncertainty is unsettling. I deserve clarity, and I believe that's a fair request."*

Rohil hesitated, *"Honestly? I haven't thought about marriage. My career is still unstable. I need to figure things out first."* Rohil faltered, trying to navigate the tense moment. This was exactly why he dreaded conversations like these—once they reached that point, his defenses began to crumble, leaving him exposed and vulnerable.

"Unstable?" She let out a short, humorless laugh. *"You just bought a new house, a new car, got a promotion, a hefty pay package. What exactly are you waiting more for?"*

Rohil stumbled over his words, his mind racing as he tried to find the right response, feeling the weight of the conversation pressing down on him.

"I want something bigger, Mysha. Becoming Chief Technology Officer (CTO)? That'll happen I know. But even that won't be enough.

There's something more, something I need to chase—something that will finally quiet this hunger inside me." The statement slipped from Rohil's lips like a glimpse into his subconscious, a fleeting truth he hadn't fully realized himself. It was as if his mind, unbidden, revealed what his heart had been hiding all along.

Mysha crossed her arms, her frustration mounting. As though his wavering on the issue of marriage wasn't enough, now his indecisiveness about his career was just the final blow—like the icing on a very unpleasant cake.

"If you don't even know what you're looking for, how will you ever find it?" Mysha challenged. *"People who want something different don't wait—they take the leap. Look at Abeer. He knew exactly what he wanted and there he is preparing for The Frozen Himalayan competition."*

At Abeer's name, something shifted in Rohil. His body tensed, his expression darkened. *"Abeer?"* His voice carried a mocking edge. *"He ran away because he couldn't handle office stress. He wouldn't have lasted a day in my position."*

Mysha knew this reaction well. Abeer had always been a sore spot for Rohil, and she played the card deliberately.

"If you were doing something extraordinary like Abeer, I might have understood. But you're in a routine software job, Rohil. And yet, you're dodging the idea of marriage. That makes me question your intentions." Mysha's voice was firm. *"Sometimes, you just have to take that leap."*

Rohil's jaw tightened. Without another word, he turned and walked away. Abeer's name had dragged something to the surface, something buried deep beneath his ambitions. As he strode toward the car, anger and hurt simmered inside him.

"If you don't trust me, then keep doubting," Rohil muttered under his breath. *"And keep admiring Abeer for his cowardly choice to*

quit the job." He shook his head, exhaling sharply. *"Great! You just ruined a perfectly good evening."*

Emotionally exposed, Mysha's eyes welled up with tears, stung by Rohil's razor-sharp remark. It cut deeper than she expected, leaving her raw and vulnerable in a way she hadn't anticipated. This weight of their emotions clung to the air between them.

The SUV cut through the silence of the highway, its headlights slicing the dark. Rohil gripped the wheel, his gaze fixed straight ahead. Mysha stared out of the window, her reflection barely visible against the glass. Neither of them spoke.

The office building buzzed with its usual morning rhythm—keyboards clacking, voices blending into an indistinct hum, the occasional ring of a phone. Rohil stepped into the lift, shoulders stiff, his jaw set in a permanent clench. Lately, everything irritated him—small mistakes, trivial inconveniences, even the way people breathed around him. It wasn't just frustration; it was a simmering uncontrollable rage clawing at him from the inside. And today was no different.

The doors slid shut, and the lift lurched upward—until it didn't. With a sudden jolt it stopped midway, the overhead lights flickering. Silence followed, thick and suffocating. Rohil pressed the alarm button, nothing happened. He pulled out his phone, his breath quickening but there was no signal. His fingers curled around the device before he shoved it into his pocket with a curse. His heartbeat drummed in his ears—not from fear but from pure undiluted irritation. How could this happen to *him*? His day had barely started and already the universe seemed to be conspiring against him.

He slammed his palm against the metal doors then kicked them hard, the clang echoing in the confined space. Again and again the rage inside him needed an outlet and this lifeless metal box became the perfect target.

From the other side a voice rang out, muffled but clear enough.

"Stay calm! The lift will open soon. No need to create a scene."

Rohil wasn't interested in patience. *"Open the damn door!"* he barked, fury lacing every word.

A heavy groan of metal followed as the security guard manually pried the doors open. Rohil stormed out his anger now squarely aimed at the uniformed man standing before him.

"Do you people even bother with maintenance? Or do you just wait for things to break before you move a finger?" His voice was sharp, cutting, demanding someone to take the blame.

The guard, already irked by his tone, scoffed. *"Not my job to fix lifts. That's for the maintenance guys. If you have a problem, go yell at someone in the office. Don't take it out on me."*

That was it. The final spark. Rohil grabbed the guard by the collar, his grip tight, his breath heavy. *"You are my problem,"* he hissed. *"And I'll make sure you don't forget it henceforth."*

The air around them thickened with tension. People began gathering, their murmurs rippling through the office lobby. A few colleagues rushed in, prying Rohil away before things spiraled beyond control.

"Let it go, Rohil," one of them urged, voice steady. *"This isn't worth it."*

The guard straightened his uniform, shaking with indignation. *"I'm not afraid of you or this job! There's plenty of land in my village—I can always go back to farming and live a better life. This job is just a way to pass the time."* He muttered under his breath, *"Putting hands on my collar? Who the hell does he think he is?"*

Rohil's colleagues pulled him away, but the fury in his veins refused to settle. He stormed past the lobby, his pulse pounding, fists clenched so tightly his nails dug into his palms. But beneath the anger something else lurked—something raw, something deeper. Something even he didn't fully understand. ---

The corporate world once a place of ambition and structure for Rohil, now felt like an endless loop of monotony. He had lost interest in the usual rituals—the morning canteen banter, the casual camaraderie with his team. Instead, he withdrew into his office, shutting out the world, drawing the curtains, and mindlessly tapping away at a games on his phone. His once open-door policy had become a thing of the past; now, he was more a ghost than a leader.

A sharp knock broke through his self-imposed solitude. Without waiting for permission, Unni stepped in, his urgency palpable.

"The new prototype's trial run needs to happen. When should we schedule it?"

Rohil, without lifting his gaze from the screen, remained engrossed in his game. *"Not now, man. It's just a prototype. The trial isn't running away. We'll get to it."*

A mounting pressure was evident in Unni's voice. *"But we can't move forward without your approval. You know there's a looming deadline. It's urgent."*

Rohil ignored him, as if nothing mattered anymore. Without looking up, he muttered, *"No big deal. The world won't end if we don't do the trial run today."*

Unni's lips pressed into a thin line. He didn't like Rohil's casual stance but there wasn't much he could do about it. He exhaled sharply. *"If Abeer were here, he'd have made sure it got done. He'd drop everything and prioritize the prototype."*

Rohil's fingers hovered over his phone screen. The mention of Abeer struck a nerve. He looked up, meeting Unni's knowing gaze. It was a challenge, a calculated jab by Unni to shake him out of his apathy. Rohil realized his behavior was starting to show cracks—his team was noticing and that wasn't good. With a reluctant sigh, he held out his hand. *"Alright. Show me."*

Unni smirked, sensing his victory. He handed over the laptop, nudging Rohil just a little further. *"Like it or not, you miss Abeer."*

Rohil scoffed, now regaining some control over himself. He leaned back and threw in a dry mocking comment. *"What is he my girlfriend? Why would I miss him?"*

Unni chuckled, undeterred. *"Funny how your brain kicks into gear the second I mention him. I swear, I could get you to do anything by using Abeer's name."*

Rohil's amusement vanished. Realizing he'd been played by his own subordinate didn't sit well with him. His face darkened. *"Shut up, Unni,"* he snapped.

Even as he spoke, he realized he had overreacted. His frustration, his restlessness—it was all bleeding through, making him too easy to read. He needed to steer the conversation elsewhere before it unraveled completely.

"It's just Mysha. We had a fight. That's why I'm in a bad mood."

Unni, ever perceptive leaned against the desk, his tone light but pointed. *"Oh yeah? She is moving out and will be staying with Komal. Living in, now separating out. That's rough."*

Rohil's jaw tensed. He didn't like Unni digging into his personal life. *"Are you done with the interrogation? Get out."*

Unni smirked, knowing he had achieved his real goal—getting Rohil to agree to the prototype trial run. Without another word, he turned and walked out, leaving behind a boss-friend who was harder to manage than most—but not impossible.

A JOURNEY BACK TO WHAT MATTERS

Rohil's apartment was dimly lit, the soft glow of the television flickering across the room. He sat on the couch, eyes fixed on the screen, but his mind elsewhere. In the bedroom Mysha silently packed her bags, the rustling of clothes and the occasional zip of her suitcase the only sounds breaking the heavy silence between them. Neither spoke, neither looked at the other. When she was finally done she stepped out dragging her luggage behind her, her presence a quiet storm passing through the room. Without a word or a glance, she walked out the door.

Minutes later, Rohil stood by the window, his hands clenched into fists as he watched Mysha settle into Komal's car. The engine hummed to life, red taillights glowing like a final goodbye before disappearing into the night. A surge of frustration shot through him, a mix of anger and helplessness tightening in his chest. Without thinking he grabbed his cell phone and hurled it onto the sofa, the soft thud of impact lost in the silence that Mysha had left behind.

Rohil's office cabin felt heavier than usual as if the walls were closing in on him. The fluorescent lights buzzed overhead, casting a sterile glow that did little to lift his spirits. His life had been unraveling ever since his breakup with Mysha; and now, it seemed his career was following the same doomed trajectory. Shoulders slumped, eyes hollow with exhaustion he sat at his desk, numbly clicking through a game on his laptop—anything to keep his mind from drowning in reality.

The door creaked open and Harish stepped in. The usual fire in his stride, the easy confidence in his voice—it was all missing. There was no need for words to know something was wrong but Harish spoke anyway, his tone edged with unease.

"Rohil, we need to stop hiring for the 'Savi Sports' app immediately," he said. *"In fact, we have to cut down at least 25% of our workforce. Savi Sports just canceled their contract. They don't need us to develop their app anymore. And to top it off, our third-quarter results look bad. If we don't act now, we won't last long."*

Rohil felt the words land like blows, each one pushing him deeper into the abyss he had been trying so hard to climb out of. *When it rains, it pours*—his life was the perfect proof. He sat there motionless, his body in the room but his mind drifting somewhere far beyond the walls of his office.

"Sir," he finally murmured, his voice stripped of all emotion, *"my whole career is built around app development. I've given up my relationship, my marriage—everything for my career."*

Harish sighed, his expression a mix of sympathy and exhaustion. *"Right now, all of us are floating without an anchor,"* he admitted. *"But we're hopeful. We're close to finalizing at least three new projects. If things go well, we'll get back on our feet soon."*

Rohil, already bracing for the worst, let his pessimism take hold. *"And if those projects don't come through?"* he asked, his voice hollow.

Harish hesitated for a moment before answering. *"Then we'll have to shut down."*

Silence stretched between them. Rohil leaned back, rubbing his temples as the weight of everything pressed down on him.

Harish took a step closer, lowering his voice as if offering advice not just as a boss, but as a friend. *"Remember three things, Rohil. First, never build a relationship on conditions. Second, always keep your career options open. And third—the most important one—take a break. Step away, breathe, reset. Go on a trip, clear your mind, and come back stronger."*

With that, he smirked faintly then turned and walked out, leaving Rohil alone in the dimly lit cabin.

Rohil sat still for a moment before his gaze landed on the wall opposite him. His mountaineering photographs hung there, their edges curled with time, their glass frames dulled with dust. They were remnants of his past self—someone who once liked to chase summits instead of prototypes, someone who had dreams beyond codes and contracts.

Slowly, as if waking from a long slumber, he stood up. Pulling a handkerchief from his pocket he reached for one of the frames, unhooking it from the wall. With gentle strokes he wiped away the dust, revealing the crisp snow-capped peaks beneath. As he stared at the photograph something flickered inside him—a whisper of an old calling, a reminder of who he used to be.

At home in the fading light of late evening, Rohil sat slumped on his couch, his fingers twitching over the game controller. The screen flashed violently—gunfire, explosions, defeat after defeat. He was losing, again and again, and with each failure his frustration thickened like smoke in the air. With a growl, he flung the controller to the ground, the plastic cracking against the floor.

His hands fumbled for his phone. He called Mysha, the call didn't even ring—her phone was switched off. A strange hollowness spread inside him, an unsettling sense of being completely shut out. For a moment, he just sat there staring at the blank screen, then without thinking he grabbed his car keys and stormed out.

The drive to Komal's apartment was a blur of speeding lights and restless thoughts. By the time he reached her building, the frustration that had been simmering within him was close to boiling over. He slammed his finger against the doorbell.

The door opened. Mysha stood there.

She didn't react—not a flicker of surprise, not a trace of hesitation. Her face was calm, almost indifferent as though she had expected him all along. Then, without looking at him she turned her head and called out into the apartment.

"Komal, someone's here to see you."

Rohil clenched his jaw. *"No, Komal, I'm not here for you,"* he shot back. *"you just relax."*

Mysha left the door open and walked back inside, settling onto the couch with a book in her hands. She didn't glance at him again, didn't acknowledge his presence. The silence in the room stretched between them, thick and heavy. Making them feel like strangers sitting across from each other.

Rohil exhaled sharply and sat down. He studied her for a moment then in a voice steadier than he expected, he spoke,

"I've made up my mind—I'm going to marry you and share a lifetime of love and adventures together."

The words landed like an anchor in the still air. Mysha didn't react right away. Her fingers hovered over the pages of her book, her gaze unwavering. She let the silence linger and allowed him to sit with his own words.

Rohil leaned forward slightly. *"But there's something important I need to do first,"* he added.

Something in his voice made her look up. This time there was no bravado, no drunken impulse. Just honesty. Mysha studied him for a moment, then, without a word she closed her book, got up and slid into her slippers.

As if on command her anger disappeared, dissolving like mist under the morning sun. A slow smirk tugged at her lips. *"See? How easy it is to make me happy?"* she teased. Then, with a dramatic sigh, she muttered under her breath, *"You made me move to Komal's place for no reason."*

She grabbed the handle of her suitcase and rolled it towards the door. It was already packed—like she had seen this moment coming, like she knew exactly how it would play out.

Rohil gawked at her, caught somewhere between disbelief and admiration. Her calm composure and maturity left him in awe; she had understood his predicament without adding to the chaos, and that alone spoke volumes about her grace. *"You're no longer angry with me, are you?"* he asked.

She turned, grinning. *"Nope, I was just messing with you. I know how to handle things in my favor. And anyway, for me to be truly mad at you, you'd have to do something really terrible. And I know you're not that bad. Whatever flaws you have, I'll tweak them as I see fit."* She winked. *"Now, let's go."*

Rohil sighed, standing up. *"One thing's for sure—I'll never understand women."*

Mysha tilted her head playfully, then met his gaze with a knowing smile. *"To understand us, you'd have to understand our very core. We're made of millions of atoms, each one moving and reacting in ways even science can't fully compute. My advice? Don't try to understand—just go with the flow. Don't react to our actions, just respond. And respond in a way we like."* Rohil stared at her, completely thrown off by this.

She laughed, watching the confusion settle on his face. *"What happened? Speechless?"*

He shook his head, exasperated. *"You played me well. If you can't convince, confuse—classic move."*

She grinned but didn't let him drag the conversation any further. Instead, she grabbed his arm and pulled him towards the door.

"Bye, Komal! I'm leaving!" she called out, not even turning back.

Before Rohil could process what had just happened, he found himself behind the wheel, driving away with Mysha beside him. The night was calm, the moon glowing brightly overhead—as if the universe itself had orchestrated this moment, knowing all along that this was exactly how it was meant to unfold.

CHAPTER-4

FROST AND FIRE

The press conference for the Frozen Himalayan Competition was in full swing, the air thick with anticipation. In the heart of Manali, under the glow of bright stage lights journalists, players, and spectators gathered, their breath misting in the cold air. A massive screen flickered to life displaying a montage of past competitions—glacial cliffs, perilous slopes, and battered climbers who had pushed themselves to the edge of human endurance.

"Four brutal challenges stand between our contenders and glory," the MC's voice thundered through the hall, commanding everyone's attention as he laid out the details of the four contests and the intricate point system of the competition.

"Our first event is Ski Jumping—a test of speed, precision, and the sheer courage to defy gravity,

"Next in the line is Snow Climbing—scaling icy walls where one wrong move spells disaster,

"Third, Rock Climbing—strength and strategy against nature's toughest obstacles. Each of these earns winner a single point.

"But the final challenge..." The MC's voice lowered, drawing the

room in.

"The Grand Marathon Climb—a merciless fusion of all three, demanding every ounce of skill, stamina, and willpower. The winner of this ultimate test earns two points, bringing the competition's total to five. The climber with the highest score claims the title of Frozen Himalayan Champion."

A hush settled over the audience as the weight of the competition sank in. Faces tensed. A few competitors exchanged knowing glances, silent acknowledgments of the dangers that awaited.

The MC continued, his tone edged with dark amusement. *"Last year, five climbers lost fingers to frostbite. Three required extensive plastic surgery after suffering burns from extreme cold. This is not just a contest— It is the ultimate test of survival of the fittest.*

"Let's leave the chills behind and move on!" the MC declared with a smirk. *"Now, allow me to introduce the ferocious warriors courageous enough to embrace this challenge."*

The first name rang through the hall. *"Bruno Botta, reigning champion from Switzerland!"* A rugged man with deep scars across his cheek stepped forward, his steely eyes revealing countless battles with the mountain.

"Next, from India—Abeer Singh!" The hall erupted into cheers. In one corner, Neet and her students clapped enthusiastically, their excitement infectious. Abeer stepped onto the stage his posture relaxed but his gaze sharp.

One by one, the rest followed—Max King from Australia, Toby Wolf from Germany, Zak Speed from the UK, Ace Light from America. Each name carried the weight of reputation, each competitor a legend in their own right.

Then came a name that made Abeer's blood run cold.

"Rohil Dhoot, from India."

A slow, deliberate clap echoed through the hall as Rohil strode onto the stage. His smirk was barely concealed, his presence laced with arrogance. He stopped beside Abeer, leaning in just enough for his words to slip through the noise.

"You didn't think I'd let you off so easily, did you, Mr. Champion?"

Abeer didn't flinch. He turned, his voice calm but laced with steel.

"Lions don't chase. They hunt. And chasing… that's for jackals like you—the ones who feed off a lion's scraps."

Rohil chuckled, his confidence unshaken.

"Who the real lion is—we'll soon find out."

Abeer smirked, tilting his head slightly.

"You've always been good at stealing, Rohil. But if you steal a glance to your left, you'll see the real king standing right beside you." Abeer said, referring to himself.

Before Rohil could respond, the MC's voice boomed over the speakers. *"And so, the countdown begins for the Frozen Himalayan Competition!"*

Applause erupted, the hall alive with excitement but beneath the celebration an invisible battle line had already been drawn. Abeer's gaze flickered to the crowd where familiar voices called his name.

"Abeer! Abeer!" Mysha, Unni, and Komal waved enthusiastically, their faces lit with excitement.

He raised a hand in acknowledgment but his focus returned to Rohil, who wore a knowing smile.

"Brought your whole team, I see," Abeer said, his tone edged with challenge.

Rohil's smile widened. *"Abeer, did you ever wonder why you could never beat me back in the office?"*

Abeer's jaw tightened, he made a snide remark. *"Would you care to enlighten me on this?"*

Rohil fired back with a sarcastic response, *"Because you never knew how to hold a team together. You always walked alone. And one man alone—"* Rohil leaned in slightly, *"—can never accomplish anything."*

Abeer's expression remained unreadable but his words cut sharp.

"You don't love your team it's just a farce, Rohil. You use them. And that's why, when the storm hits you'll find yourself standing alone."

Rohil scoffed, but before he could retort, Mysha, Unni, and Komal stepped onto the stage, shook hands with Abeer and wished him good luck. Beneath the polite exchanges and forced smiles, the real battle had already begun.

Two rivals, once corporate adversaries, now warriors on ice and rock, ready to face the most unforgiving challenge of their lives. The Frozen Himalayas wouldn't just test their strength—it would test their very survival.

TACTICAL ASCENT

Rohil ran his operations for competition like a corporation. His makeshift gym-office in Manali wasn't just a training space; it was a war room. Every piece of equipment, every file, every meeting had a singular focus—winning. Unni, Komal, and Mysha, his core team, had worked tirelessly for weeks, researching every potential threat in the competition. Now, it was time to go over their findings.

Unni pressed a button on the remote and the projector flickered to life. The screen filled with the imposing image of 'Bruno Botta' mid-climb, his muscles taut as he ascended a sheer rock face.

"This guy is the strongest competitor in the tournament," Unni said, his voice carrying the weight of their research. *"Out of ten competitions, he's only lost once.*

Rohil smirked as his gaze shifted back to the screen, where Botta was now shown maneuvering through a series of grueling adventure sports—free climbing, base jumping, ice scaling. The guy was a machine. Rohil's smile faded.

"What's his biggest strength?" Rohil asked, his tone now serious.

"His greatest strength is being cunning." Unni replied. *"The guy's ruthless. He plays dirty—While climbing, he deliberately knocks loose rocks down to hit the climbers below."*

"That's unethical!" Rohil protested. *"Shouldn't someone file a complaint?"*

"They do," Unni shrugged. *"But he always denies it. 'Did anyone see me do it?' That remains Botta's resolute defense as he dismisses every accusation thrown his way."*

Rohil scowled. *"Crooked bastard."*

"That's how he stays number one." Unni replied with a condescending sneer.

Rohil leaned back in his chair, lost in thought. Just then, Mysha entered, setting her bag down and heading straight for the coffee machine. The room was tense, thick with unspoken strategies. She poured herself a cup, then slid into a seat beside Rohil.

"The best adventure sports trainer in India is Neet," she said casually, stirring her coffee. *"She works at the Indian Climbing Institute."*

Rohil's focus sharpened in an instant. A breakthrough. *"Hire her immediately."* Rohil commanded.

"She won't train you," Mysha said, unfazed.

Rohil frowned. *"Why not? We'll offer double her fee."*

Mysha hesitated, then lowered her voice as if spilling a secret.

"Because she's Abeer's girlfriend. And she's already training him... unofficially."

For a second, Rohil didn't move. Then, slowly, he stood up. A moment ago, this was just about hiring the best trainer. But now, knowing Neet's connection to Abeer, the situation transformed into something much bigger. Rohil never acted unless a single move created multiple ripple effects. And this—this was the perfect opportunity. If he hired Neet, he wouldn't just weaken Abeer's training—he'd plant a seed of discord between Abeer and Neet, creating tension in their relationship. That stress would weigh on Abeer, affecting his focus and performance in the competition, giving Rohil a decisive edge. The competition wouldn't just be won on the mountain—it would be won right here, in this room.

Rohil turned to Mysha, his voice calm but decisive. *"Set up a meeting with the institute's dean."*

She narrowed her eyes. *"Why?"*

Rohil smirked. *"An institute needs funding to run. We'll make Neet's training official."*

This was no longer just about victory. It was about controlling the entire game.

In the neat yet imposing office of the Dean at ICI (Indian climbing Institute), Rohil and Mysha sat across from the man who held the power to finalize their most crucial decision. The air hummed with quiet expectation as Mysha, ever meticulous signed the cheque that would seal their arrangement. The Dean, a man who rarely expressed more than what was necessary, looked undeniably pleased. With a decisive nod he approved the hiring of Neet as Rohil's trainer.

"Neet is one of the most sincere, hardworking, and talented trainers in the country," the Dean stated, his voice carrying the weight of deep respect.

"That's exactly why we came to you," Rohil responded smoothly, his confidence solid.

Mysha glanced up from the cheque her lips curving into a knowing smirk. She had learned to read Rohil well, and this particular choice of words intrigued her. The Dean, however, remained focused, his admiration for Neet evident.

"She's not the kind to take on just any player," he continued. *"Neet won't agree unless she's absolutely convinced of your dedication.*

From your workouts to your sleep schedule, she'll dictate it all. You'll follow her rules, no exceptions."

At that very moment the door creaked open and Neet walked in. Her posture was upright, her expression composed but distant. There was something unreadable in her eyes, as though she had already made up her mind about all of this. The Dean gestured toward her with a welcoming nod.

"Hey! Neet, meet Mr. Rohil."

Rohil stood, extending a hand his signature warm smile in place.

"Welcome aboard, Neet. We're honored to have you as part of the team."

Neet's fingers brushed his in a firm but fleeting handshake. Her face remained impassive, her silence heavier than words. Whatever was running through her mind, she kept it locked away.

The Dean sensed the subtle shift in Neet's demeanor, he cleared his throat and turned to Mysha. *"And this is Mysha, Rohil's manager."*

Mysha, ever graceful, reached out with practiced warmth. *"With you on board, our team is finally complete,"* she said smoothly. *"This gives me confidence that victory will be ours."*

Neet accepted the handshake but didn't echo the enthusiasm. Though her expression carried a reluctant smile, a quiet storm brewed beneath it. The pressure from the institute was evident, yet she held herself steady, revealing just enough to be polite but never enough to be fully understood.

The evening mist clung to the winding roads of Manali, swirling around Neet and Abeer as they walked in quiet contemplation. The distant hum of the river echoed through the valley but Neet barely heard it. Her mind was a battlefield, riddled with the impossible logistics of training both Abeer and Rohil while fulfilling her duties at ICI. There were only so many hours in a day and no matter how she rearranged them something always fell through the cracks. The weight of responsibility pressed heavy on her chest.

Abeer, ever observant, stole a glance at her furrowed brow and restless energy. He knew her well enough to recognize when she was stuck in a loop of overthinking.

"When a puzzle doesn't fit you don't force it," he mused, his tone light but deliberate. *"You take out the pieces that don't belong."*

Neet scoffed, rolling her eyes. *"Great. I'll just quit my job, then."*

Abeer smirked, unfazed and tapped into the flaw in her reasoning .

"In your statement you got word 'quit' right. The word 'job' is where you went wrong."

She shot him an unimpressed look. *"Oh, but it's perfect. If I quit, I won't have to train Rohil. Problem solved."* Her sarcasm didn't mask her frustration and Abeer knew better than to push too hard too soon. Instead, he let her talk.

"The institute remains resolute," she continued. "They want me to train Rohil exclusively for the competition."

At this, Abeer let out a quiet, knowing breath. *"Rohil Dhoot,"* he muttered, more to himself than to her. His jaw tensed slightly, and there was something in his voice—an edge Neet hadn't expected. *"If he's here, trouble isn't far behind."*

She frowned, turning to him. *"You sound like you know him."*

Abeer's smirk returned, but it didn't reach his eyes. *"I don't just know him. I know his kind. The smooth talkers. The schemers."* He exhaled sharply, shaking his head. *"He is that same office guy I was telling you about; shrewd, calculated."*

Neet blinked, the pieces clicking into place. Her expression hardened. *"Ahh! Now I get it. Thanks for helping me make up my mind—I'm definitely not training him."*

A silence stretched between them as the road curved through the hills, the mist thickening, swallowing the world around them. For a while, only the sound of their footsteps filled the empty space.

Then, just as she thought the conversation was over, Abeer spoke again. *"Actually you should train him."*

Neet came to an abrupt halt, spinning to face him. *"What?"* She narrowed her eyes. *"Abeer, you've legitimately lost it."*

His voice remained calm, steady. *"Neet, you're my girlfriend. If you refuse to train him, it'll look like I'm the one holding you back—like I'm insecure, afraid to let you be around him. But that's not who I am. I don't need to prove I'm the best—I know I am. And nothing, no one can shake that."*

Neet crossed her arms. "And what about my responsibility towards you?" Her voice softened slightly but her conviction remained. *"Training him would feel like a betrayal."*

Abeer let out a short laugh, shaking his head. *"Training is your job and training Rohil?"* He raised a brow. *"That's the real challenge. Anyone can train a natural athlete like me, but molding an underdog like Rohil into a champion—that takes real skill."*

Neet's expression didn't waver. *"I never signed up to create champions, so spare me the speech—I'm not interested."*

    "Maybe not," Abeer conceded. *"But Rohil is different. He's sharp, Neet. He learns fast. He has the ability to master things quicker than most. He just needs the right guidance. Trust me, he's going to surprise you."*

    "I don't care," she shot back.

Their conversation had shifted from a disagreement to a full-fledged standoff. The air around them felt heavier, charged.

Abeer's tone turned firm. *"Then I'll have no choice but to fire you from my training program."*

Neet's mouth parted in disbelief. *"Has anyone ever told you that you're a complete psycho?"*

His smirk was immediate. *"Nope. Never."*

"Well, congratulations. I'm telling you now. Make a note of it."

Despite her irritation, she knew one thing—Abeer was serious. He meant every word. No amount of arguing would change his mind.

They walked on, the silence between them stretching as the mist thickened, obscuring the road ahead. Finally, Abeer broke the quiet his voice softer this time. *"Think of it this way—you're not just training some guy. You'd be giving India another world-class climber. Climbing isn't just a job for you, Neet—it's your passion as well. Do something for climbing, nurture new talent. Think of it as giving back to the sport you love."*

She let out a long, measured breath, her resolve wavering just slightly. *"Don't try to be too clever, Abeer. Let me think about it."*

With that, they disappeared into the fog, their figures swallowed by the shifting landscape. In the mountains, the weather turned in an instant—one moment, a serene calm; the next, a brewing storm. And so it was with people, with choices, with the ever-changing balance of relationships.

CHAPTER-5

GRIT OVER STRENGTH

Rohil sat in his gym-office his fingers tapping idly against the desk, while behind him Mysha, Unni, and Komal scribbled notes, their pens moving in quick deliberate strokes. At the front of the room Neet stood with a commanding presence, a collection of X-ray scans spread before her, the glow of the projector casting shifting shadows across her face. The touchscreen displayed the entire mountain range, a frozen world of jagged peaks and treacherous slopes. With a single swipe of her finger, Neet zoomed in, isolating a specific section. She circled the area her voice steady, calculated.

"This is where all the competitions take place," she said as new images flickered onto the screen. *"Right here, because this spot is unlike any other—rock faces, snow-covered peaks, a skiing slope, and high-lining cliffs all crammed into one brutal arena."*

With another command the screen shifted, revealing an X-ray view of the towering rock formations. The image zoomed deeper, past the imposing façade into the very particles that held the mountain together. Neet's expression was unreadable as she spoke.

"This is one of the deadliest rock faces in the world. It's not solid—it's made of millions of loose stones barely balanced on top of one another. One misplaced grip, one careless move and the entire section collapses, taking the climber with it. And if that isn't bad enough, imagine this in the middle of a downpour."

A heavy silence settled over the room. Mysha swallowed hard. Unni's pen stopped moving.

Then, the screen transitioned, revealing what looked like a blank white expanse. *"And this?"* Neet continued, her voice unfaltering. *"This isn't just an empty white screen. It's fog. And you'll be skiing through it."*

"No way," Mysha murmured, her voice barely above a whisper.

The screen flickered again, morphing into a simulation. As the thick fog lifted, a new nightmare was unveiled—a ski slope lined with towering trees, their dark silhouettes standing like silent sentinels. Neet's gaze flickered toward Rohil.

"You'll be no better than blind," she said. *"At 100 kilometers per hour, you won't see the trees until the last second. One wrong decision, one moment of hesitation and it's not about winning or losing anymore—it's about life and death."*

The image shifted again, this time focusing on a snow-covered peak. *"And this,"* Neet said, *"looks like snow, doesn't it?"* She zoomed in, layer by layer, the white mass peeling away until its true nature was revealed. *"When you get close, you'll see—it's a frozen waterfall. In some parts, you can even make out the water droplets frozen mid-fall, hanging in time."*

Mysha exhaled sharply. *"This is insanity. Who climbs on frozen water?"*

Neet let the question linger before answering. *"That's why this competition is the ultimate test of endurance for the human body and mind; it's a king of all adventure sports,"* she said. *"It's not about brute strength. It's not about how powerful your arms or legs are. The real champions are the ones with the strongest fingers and the sharpest claws."* Her eyes locked onto Rohil. *"Starting tomorrow, that's exactly what we'll be training for."*

Neet wasn't just a climber—she was a strategist, a survivor, someone who understood every ruthless detail of what lay ahead. This wasn't about scaring Rohil. It was about preparing him. Because in this world, hesitation meant falling. And falling meant failure.

The sun hung low over the boulders of Manali, casting long shadows across the uneven terrain. Neet stood at the base of a rock formation, her gaze sweeping over the rough weathered surfaces. Around her the team—Rohil, Mysha, Unni, and Komal—watched in anticipation. The area was a climber's playground, each boulder varying in difficulty, each a test of strength, technique, and willpower. Unni had his camera rolling capturing the day's practice. Below them, crash mats lay in place ready to soften any falls.

Neet turned to the group, her voice steady. *"A climber's fingers should cling to the rock like magnets. Every grip must be—"*

Before she could finish, Rohil felt an irresistible pull, as if the rock itself reached out to him—an unspoken reunion between long-lost friends drawn together by fate. He grabbed hold of the rock and with smooth precision began his ascent. No ropes. No hesitation. His movements were confident, calculated. Within moments he was at the top. When he finally climbed back down, Neet was impressed.

She pointed to a much harder boulder. *"The one you just did was V5 on the difficulty scale. Judging by your grip and technique, I think you're ready to go straight for a V12 boulder. Only the truly seasoned can climb it."*

Rohil took on the challenge. The rock was tougher, the holds smaller and midway through he slipped—three, four times—before finally reaching the top. When he came back down, his expression was unreadable still frustration lingered in his eyes.

       "I'm out of practice," he admitted. *"That's the only reason I slipped."*

Neet studied him for a moment, then nodded. *"Your grip needs to be strong enough to hold your entire body weight before you make a move. If you rush without a firm grip, you'll slip. You were too hasty this time."*

A smirk tugged at the corner of Rohil's lips. *"Just keep giving me these tips, and watch how I climb."*

Neet smirked back. She had seen enough to know—he wasn't an amateur. He didn't need basic drills. He needed to be pushed. Without reluctance, she pointed toward the next and ultimate challenge in bouldering.

"This one's the toughest—a V16 boulder." She said.

The team moved toward the C-shaped boulder, its overhang forming an intimidating obstacle. Each time Rohil reached the overhang, the tricky curve made the climb even harder. No matter how determined he was, his grip would falter sending him back onto the crash mat again and again. The frustration in his eyes deepened with every failed attempt.

Meanwhile Abeer arrived for his own training session. Seeing the V16 boulder already occupied he stopped a few steps away, folding his arms as he watched. Mysha noticed him and walked over.

"Hey, Abeer," she greeted.

He nodded in acknowledgment. *"How long is this going to take?"* He inquired.

She followed his gaze to the boulder where Rohil had just hit the mat again. *"No idea. This one's brutal. Looks like Rohil is going to take a while to master it."*

Abeer turned away, ready to leave but Mysha called after him. *"We're about to break for lunch. Stay back and eat with us."*

"No, thanks." During their lunch break, he realizes there is an opportunity to practice. Abeer walked away and sat down on the grass, waiting for his turn.

In the interim, Rohil was still at war with the overhang. Neet watched him closely analyzing his movements. His fingers clung to the rock but his footwork faltered, the two moving in discord. Each pause before a slip betrayed his exhaustion, a silent struggle playing out in every hesitant grip and misplaced step.

"I think we should try again after lunch," she said finally. *"You're drained."*

As Neet turned away her eyes landed on Abeer. A grin spread across her face and she ran toward him throwing her arms around him. Neet is in a mood to engage in playful charm and lighthearted banter. Takes a dig at Abeer.

"Ah! You came to surprise me, huh?"

Abeer barely reacted. His expression was tense, his shoulders rigid. *"Come on, Neet. The competition is around the corner, and you're playing around. I'm here to train."*

Neet chuckled, undeterred. *"Sometimes, you have to lie a little to make others happy. Being serious is good, but being in competition mode twenty-four-seven? That's just insanity."*

Abeer exhaled sharply, the ghost of a smirk playing at his lips. *"I refuse to offer hollow happiness. When it comes to competition, victory isn't just about effort—it demands obsession."* Abeer clarify his position discreetly.

Just then Rohil approached, his gaze flicking between the two before extending a hand to Abeer. They shook, but his next words were pointed. *"Sorry, bro. I stole your trainer."* He said pointing at Neet.

Setting up the lunch table, Mysha scoffed in disgust. *"That's a mean thing to say, Rohil."*

But Abeer wasn't offended. He met Mysha's gaze calmly. *"This is between two athletes, Mysha. Don't worry—we'll settle it our way."*

Abeer turned back to Rohil. With his deep baritone voice, he spoke with authority. *"You can't play the game until you've gathered all the best things that truly matter—let alone people—for yourself, can you?"*

Rohil chuckled. *"Best things always gives you an edge. It makes you powerful. It pushes you to deliver your absolute best."*

Abeer's expression darkened. *"Your judgment seems off that's not power. That's a distraction. If you focused as much on training as you do on hoarding the best, you'd have climbed that boulder by now. Power breeds arrogance."*

Rohil clenched his jaw. The sting of failing the boulder was nothing compared to Abeer pointing it out.

Abeer turned his gaze to the towering rock. *"Look at that rock. Nothing is stronger, nothing more massive. And yet, it never flaunts its power. When snow falls, it turns cold. When it rains, it becomes wet. It adapts to its surroundings without losing its essence. That is real power."*

Something inside Rohil snapped. *"Enough with the metaphors,"* he growled. *"I'm here to defeat you. I'll shatter every one of your fancy words so you'll have none left."*

Abeer only smiled and walked away.

As the team settled in for lunch, Neet glanced over and saw Abeer approaching the V16 boulder. Instinctively, she moved beneath, ready to guide him in case of a fall.

Abeer reached the overhang—where Rohil had repeatedly failed. Hanging upside down at the tip of the curvature he executed a seamless flip. Shifting into a straight position as he gripped the rock with his hands, freeing his legs. It was a maneuver few would dare attempt. He pulled it off effortlessly.

Silence.

Rohil sprang to his feet and launched himself at the boulder, determination fueling every move. Without thinking, he attempted the Abeer's move and this time—he succeeded to climb the overhang part. Neet stared, caught between awe and disbelief.

Though Abeer and Rohil were rivals, Abeer had the maturity to acknowledge talent. If anything, Fierce competition always ignited his drive, pushing him to deliver his very best.

Abeer paused while packing up his gear and glanced at Neet, who was assisting him. *"Told you. He just needed the right training."*

Neet, however, had a different insight. *"Not technique—mental training. Without that, he'll never match you."*

Since Neet now officially belonged to Rohil's team, Abeer couldn't resist a jab at her girlfriend. Abeer arched a brow, *"Train him however you want. The winds of victory are blowing my way."*

Neet matched move for move, giving as good as she got. *"Winds change direction in an instant, love. Hope you're ready for the storm."*

They shared a lingering look, filled with unspoken admiration—the kind only two souls in love could understand. Abeer pulled her into a warm embrace, his voice gentle yet firm as he whispered, "All the best—to you and your team."

And with that, he walked away, leaving behind the unmistakable charge of a battle yet to come.

FORGED BY THE MOUNTAIN

As the competition loomed closer training grew more grueling. Under Neet's unrelenting guidance Rohil's endurance was stretched to its breaking point. Before the first light of dawn, the team gathered at the base of the flat rock face—Neet, Rohil, Mysha, and the others. Rohil tilted his head back taking in the structure of the rock, it's seemed an easy target. A smirk played on his lips.

"Come on, Neet. Even Unni could climb this," he quipped, his tone laced with sarcasm.

Neet didn't respond. Instead she reached into her pocket, pulled out a blindfold and tied it over Rohil's eyes.

"If it's that easy, then climb," she challenged.

Rohil hesitated. His confidence wavered—not that he'd admit it. Instead, he masked his unease with words. *"If you tie a man's hands and feet and throw him into the ocean, telling him to swim, he's bound to drown."*

Neet, ever the firm believer in adaptation turned towards Rohil and shared an insight with him.

"The human body is extraordinary. When one sense fails, the others sharpen to compensate. Your touch, your hearing, even the way your muscles register space—they all work together. If you trust your body, it will guide you. My only advice? Communicate with every part of yourself. Listen. React. Adapt."

Mysha, Unni, and Komal exchanged glances, struck by the weight of her words.

Neet stepped closer to Rohil, lowering her voice. *"You have to mold yourself to the mountain. The mountain will never bend for you."*

She guided him to the base of the rock, placing his hands against its rough, weathered surface. Rohil swallowed hard. Deprived of sight, the climb felt impossibly foreign. His fingers sought purchase, his feet scraped for a firm hold. With sheer determination he managed to ascend a few feet—but the moment his footing faltered, gravity took him down. His body slammed against the rock, scraping his arms and knees. He landed hard, breath ragged, skin burning.

Neet stood over him, expression unreadable. *"You have one month to conquer this climb. By the end of your training, you should be able to scale this rock blindfolded. It's your true test. If you fail—then pack your bags and return to the corporate world. The mountains aren't meant for you."*

Rohil's chest heaved, exhaustion pressing down on him. The weight of her expectations felt unbearable. But he wasn't one to quit. A fire burned inside him—hot, unyielding. And at the center of that fire was *Abeer*. His name alone was enough to send adrenaline coursing through Rohil's veins. He clenched his fists, jaw tightening.

"Do you think Abeer can do it?" he asked, voice rough.

Neet smiled. *"Not 'can,' Rohil. He already is— every day, twice a day."*

Somewhere, far from here, Abeer was in the midst of his own climb. His body moved with an almost inhuman precision, each muscle tuned to the rock beneath him. Blindfolded, he scaled the jagged surface as if he were a part of it, his breath steady despite the punishing ascent. Even for someone of his skill the terrain was merciless. His foot slipped, his skin scraped raw against the unforgiving stone. Blood smeared against the rock—but he didn't falter. He kept climbing. Higher. Stronger. Unremitting.

Neet's voice echoed in Rohil's mind. *"With nature as your opponent, you can never truly master mountaineering. But Abeer—he's different. His mind is flexible. He adapts. He has trained himself to endure pain in ways most people can't even fathom. If you want to stand a chance against him, you need to work harder. And faster."*

Something inside Rohil snapped. Neet was underestimating him. Doubting him. He could endure a lot—but being seen as *less*? That, he would never accept. His pride burned, muscles tensed and in that moment, failure was no longer an option.

In the Frozen Himalayan Competition, physical strength was just one side of the coin—mental endurance was what truly separated winners from losers, survivors from those who succumbed to the elements. Time and again, climbers found themselves in situations where a single moment of hesitation could mean the difference between victory and failure, life and death. Neet's training program was designed to prepare her team for both—the body had to be strong, but the mind had to be even stronger.

At the gym, Neet handed Rohil two bottles of milk, each weighing about two liters, instructing him to hold them at arm's length and keep his arms steady. Rohil, now accustomed to Neet's unconventional methods, expected something brutal and mind-bending, not what seemed like a childish challenge. With a smirk, he scoffed, *"This is a climbing competition, not a milk-drinking contest. You've literally handed me baby bottles."*

Neet, a seasoned climber who had no patience for arrogance, gave him a level stare. *"To make you a real climber, I need to break your baby teeth first. This competition isn't won by brute strength but by a powerful mind."*

Mysha chuckled, knowing how difficult it was to handle Rohil's ego. But Neet—strong, unwavering—made it clear who was in charge. There was no room for negotiation.

Rohil, still amused, assumed the task would be effortless. But within minutes, his arms began to tremble, his muscles screaming in protest. A searing pain shot through his shoulders, and before he could stop himself, his hands dropped. Neet let out an unimpressed smirk.

"That's it? Not even two minutes?" she mocked.

Handing over the stopwatch to Rohil, she picked up the bottles herself, stretched her arms, and held them steady. One minute passed. Two. Five. She finally put them down and pointed at Rohil's biceps, then at his head. *"Your arm strength is hollow because your mind is filled with nonsense. Forget about matching me—you couldn't even last half my time. Hone your mind like a blade, or be chased out like a cornered rat."*

Rohil clenched his fists. His blood boiled at her constant jabs. His pride had taken a serious hit. *"No one talks to me like this."* He made it clear.

Neet didn't flinch. *"I will. And if you don't perform, you'll be humiliated. If you want to avoid that, prove yourself."*

She knew exactly what she was doing. Rohil's ego was fragile, but that was what made it a perfect weapon—she was using it against him, forcing him to push beyond his limits. She believed humans had an untapped reservoir of strength. When a person teeters on the edge of their breaking point believing they can endure no more, a resilient mind can transform that very edge into a threshold—an opening to something new, a chance to rise from the ruins and begin again.

But right now, Rohil was drained, physically and mentally. He stormed off to a chair, fuming. Unni and Komal tried to calm him down, but nothing stung more than being humiliated by Neet in front of everyone. Worse, she wasn't even sparing him a glance. She had already moved on.

At the cycling bay, she stood beside an advanced exercise bike equipped with scientific monitoring devices. She checked her watch, silently pressuring him to come over. Rohil seethed but he had no choice. Swallowing his pride, he walked up and sat on the bike. Without wasting a second, Neet began explaining.

"Your muscles have far more power than you think. It's your weak mind that gives up first. If you want to survive the extreme conditions of this competition, your mind has to be stronger than your body. The moment your mind surrenders, you're out."

Rohil rolled his eyes. *"And cycling is supposed to make my mind sharper?"*

Neet shut down his sarcasm with a single instruction. *"Just do it."*

Hooked up to various monitors—heart rate sensors, oxygen masks, pulse calculators—Rohil began pedaling. A virtual race appeared on the screen in front of him. His digital opponent was swift, unrelenting, always ahead. He pushed harder, breath ragged, legs screaming for relief. He managed to cover 10 kilometers in 15 minutes—what he thought was a decent score.

Gasping, he looked at Neet expecting at least a nod of approval. Instead, she turned away unimpressed. Before leaving the room she dropped her final command. *"We'll do this again in an hour, after lunch. Be ready."*

The door shut behind her and whatever restraint Rohil had been holding onto snapped. *"She is so arrogant and difficult human being,."* Rohil smirk. *" Perfect for Abeer,"* he muttered bitterly.

Mysha, watching everything unfold grinned. *"Nope. She's perfect for you. She knows exactly how to rein in a wild spirit like yours."*

"Perfect, my foot," Rohil grumbled, storming off, his pride in shambles, but his determination burning hotter than ever.

The day started early for Rohil and his team, as always. Lunch was their only moment of respite but today an uneasy silence loomed over the table. Rahul's absence was palpable, casting a morbid shadow over the group.

While the others refueled, Rohil was at cycling bay—pushing himself past limits that should have stopped him long ago. He refused to step off the bicycle, his legs a relentless machine, pedaling with unyielding determination. Sweat dripped from his face, his breath ragged, his body screaming for rest. Every one of his vitals blinked red on the monitor but he ignored the warning signs.

Then, without warning, Neet strode in and yanked the emergency stop tag. The bike ground to a halt, nearly throwing Rohil forward. He barely had the strength to glare at her before she started her tirade.

"I gave you an hour to recuperate, Rohil! And here you are pushing yourself to the brink. Our next exercise demands you to be fresh, and now thanks to your stubbornness, we have to waste another hour just to cool you down. Do you even realize what you're doing to yourself?"

Rohil, still panting, wiped the sweat from his brow and met her gaze with fierce defiance. His voice though hoarse was steady.

"This is the freshest I'll ever be," he said, chest heaving. *"You think I'm done? Throw a challenge at me and watch—I'll prove you wrong."*

Neet crossed her arms, her expression unreadable for a moment. Then with a smirk that carried both amusement and challenge, she leaned in slightly.

"Alright, Rohil. Let's shatter every wrong notion you've wrapped yourself in."

At the gym, Rohil mounted the stationary bike once again, his fingers tightening around the handles as digital sensors flickered to life once again. The screen in front of him displayed two figures—one in red, the other in blue—both pedaling through a breathtaking virtual landscape. Neet, standing beside him, pointed at the red figure.

"That's you from your first race," she explained. Then, she gestured at the blue. *"And this is you now. Today, your challenge is to race against your past self."*

Rohil raised a brow. *"Seriously? When you ran out of opponents to challenge me with, you decided to pit me against myself?"*

Neet smirked. *"Exactly. Last time, you covered 10 kilometers in 15 minutes. Honestly, I don't expect you to even reach 8 kilometers this time."*

Her words struck a nerve. Rohil didn't just dislike losing—he despised it. And the thought of being beaten by his own past self? Unthinkable. *"I don't lose,"* he said, his voice steady. *"Not to anyone. And definitely not to myself."*

With that, he slammed his foot onto the pedal, determination flaring in his eyes. The race began, the red Rohil speeding ahead, but the blue Rohil—the present one—was obstinate. He pushed harder his muscles burning, his breath sharp, his focus steadfast. The gap between them shrank, then disappeared. And then—he was ahead.

With every second his past self faded further behind. By the time he crossed the finish line, he had shattered his own previous record. Completing the 10-kilometer circuit in just 12 minutes—three minutes faster than before.

Neet glanced at the screen, her expression unreadable, her face smooth not a single crease of surprise or concern. *"Everything was the same this time,"* she mused, *"yet within an hour, you managed to beat yourself by a solid margin of 3minutes."*

Rohil leaned back, chest throbbing, a triumphant grin spreading across his face. *"No words of praise? Didn't I tell you? I don't lose."* Rohil with a sense of pride said to Neet.

Neet, unimpressed by his arrogance, cut straight to the point. *"This little victory is just to keep your ego entertained. The real win will be when you conquer the Frozen Himalayan title. And, my friend, you're still far from that."* She held his gaze, her voice staunch. *"This wasn't about endurance. It was about the limitless power of mind —your mind won this race, not your body. Learn to harness that power of both."*

Her bluntness, as always unsettled Rohil. Lately, every conversation between them had turned into verbal duels where neither yielded an inch. *"That's an interesting theory,"* he shot back. *"But my mind is still a part of my body, isn't it?"*

Neet's smirk deepened. *"Your body may be strong, but without the mind's command, it's powerless. This time, you trained your mind not to grow, but to prove me wrong—to defeat me, to wound my ego. And that's where the real problem lies. Your mindset needs a shift. The goal should be yours, the struggle should be yours, and the victory should belong to you alone. Challenge yourself, not others. Measure progress by asking: Am I better than my previous version? If you embrace this mindset, your growth will be limitless. And the best part? You won't need a competitor or an opponent to fuel your journey."*

Rohil, never one to be outdone chuckled, *"Then maybe you should train your mind to accept something too—"* He let the words dangle.

Neet didn't miss a beat. *"That you're the champion of the Frozen Himalayan competition, right?"*

A pause. Then, she sneered, *"That was just a warm-up. Training has only just begun."*

Neet's training philosophy was unlike anything Unni and Komal had ever encountered. She combined scientific principles with spiritual wisdom, pushing boundaries in ways that seemed almost absurd to those who thought conventionally. As expected, Unni and Komal struggled to wrap their heads around it. Doubt festered between them, growing with each bizarre task Neet set before Rohil.

The next phase of training was something even more incomprehensible—understanding pain. Not just tolerating it but truly comprehending its nature, its mechanisms and how a trained mind could endure it without suffering much. For most, pain was an enemy, an unavoidable misery. But Neet knew otherwise. She had seen people who had mastered the art of detachment from pain, and now, She was about to prove it.

Their destination was a secluded monastery, nestled on a hilltop; its wisdom buried within the silence of the mountains. To reach it they had to climb 800 stone steps, an arduous ascent that quickly took its toll. As Neet led the way with unwavering energy, Unni and Komal fell behind, breathless and drained. They collapsed onto the steps, chests panting, their bodies refusing to move any further.

Rohil, who had been walking ahead turned back to check on them. Unni wiped the sweat off his forehead, struggling to catch his breath. *"I swear, Neet is just playing with us,"* he muttered between gasps.

Komal, equally exasperated, nodded. *"Yeah, she's making you do all this insane stuff just so you forget whatever climbing skills you have left with."*

Unni narrowed his eyes, suspicion flickering across his face. *"And meanwhile, Abeer is probably out there, scaling mountains and pushing himself in real-world conditions, while we waste our breath on this madness."*

Komal cast a wary glance. *"Honestly, to me this feels like some elaborate sabotage plan cooked up by Neet and Abeer. A classic boyfriend-girlfriend conspiracy to throw you off your game. Maybe they're just setting you up to fail."*

Unni let out a dry laugh. *"She's going to turn you into a monk by the end of this, Rohil."*

Before Rohil could respond Mysha approached, overhearing their whispers. She shot them a sharp look. *"Stop whining and get moving"*

Even though Rohil remained silent, their words lingered in his mind. A part of him was starting to wonder the same thing.

Finally, they reached the monastery, their legs aching from the climb. But any exhaustion they felt was instantly forgotten when their eyes landed on the scene before them.

Monks balanced upside down on their hands along the ledge of the cliff, their bodies perfectly still, suspended between earth and sky. The sheer control it required was mind-boggling, yet what truly struck them was the expression on the monks' faces. Not a single one showed strain, fear, or discomfort. Instead, they smiled—serene, at peace as if their inverted position was the most natural thing in the world.

Neet stepped forward and pointed toward them. *"This is what a trained mind looks like,"* she said, her voice calm yet powerful. *"Faces that should have been twisted with strain or darkened by the fear of falling instead glowed with quiet, unshakable joy."*

Rohil stared at them, disbelief flickering across his face.

"This level of control," Neet continued, her voice firm, *"is only possible with a mind that is calm and steady. And that kind of mastery? It comes through the discipline of meditation."*

A storm of agitation swelled in Rohil. He took a deep breath, frustration bubbling to the surface. *"Neet, one moment you're telling us to sharpen our minds—to make them quick, strong, and alert. And now you're saying we need to slow them down? You can't have it both ways!"* Rohil exclaimed, frustration flickering in his eyes.

Neet turned to him, an amused smile playing on her lips. *"See? You're simply reacting to my words instead of truly responding to them. On the surface it may seem contradictory but if you look deeper you'll understand—I'm talking about the fluidity of the mind. It shouldn't be rigid or fixed; it should flow, adjusting to whatever the moment demands, regardless of contradiction."* She paused, then added with a smirk, *"Think less, flow more—act in the moment. Only a sharp and strong mind know how to slow down"*

Mysha, who had been silently observing, nodded thoughtfully. *"I think Neet is right."*

Unni groaned. *"She's just twisting words around."*

Neet ignored him and locked eyes with Rohil as she elaborated, offering an example.

"When you're hanging thousands of feet above the ground and you slip, what will you do? If you let anger take over—if you lash out at the mountain—you will lose. That anger is just a reaction. But if, in that moment, you see an opportunity—maybe a foothold you hadn't noticed before—you might just save yourself. That will be your response."

She paused, letting her words sink in. *"Train your mind to be flexible. Because the mountains, and life, will throw the unimaginable at you. And the only thing that will determine whether you survive or fall… is how you respond."*

With that, she turned and walked ahead, leaving them to process her words. One by one, they followed, some deep in thought, others still drowning in doubt.

The monastery stood like a relic of a forgotten world untouched by the rush of technology, shielded from the noise of modernity. In an age where artificial intelligence dictated the pace of life, where human ambition and innovation intertwined to create a storm of chaos, places like this had become rare sanctuaries. Here, simplicity wasn't a choice; it was a way of being. The crisp mountain air carried the scent of ancient wisdom and even the most restless souls found themselves stilled within its walls. Rohil and his team, whether they admitted it or not, were deeply moved by what they experienced.

As they entered the central courtyard a monk silently approached and handed each of them a wooden stick. In the center, a lama sat motionless in meditation, his presence commanding yet peaceful. Rohil stood, gripping his stick when the lama lifted his gaze and spoke with a gesture. *"Strike me on the shoulder."*

Rohil hesitated before landing a light tap. Without a moment's pause, the lama rose and slapped him—hard—across the face. A stunned silence fell over the courtyard. Smiling as if nothing had happened, the lama returned to his meditative posture. Confused but intrigued, Rohil tightened his grip and struck him again, this time with force. To everyone's astonishment the lama remained unshaken, his expression unchanged.

Then, with the same serene gaze, the lama gestured for Rohil to sit. Bowing slightly, he raised his stick and struck Rohil's shoulder with full force. A sharp jolt of pain tore through Rohil, making him wince. Mysha instinctively stepped forward dragging Unni and Komal with her. But they, too, were not spared. One by one, the lama struck them, their cries of pain echoing through the courtyard.

Rohil, rubbing his sore shoulder, turned to Neet with narrowed eyes. *"So this is your idea of training? Getting us beaten up?"*

Neet smiled, unshaken by his frustration. *"This wasn't punishment—it was a lesson. Just a taste of what's to come. The training is far from over and tomorrow it will push you even further. Pain will be your teacher and trust me you'll remember every part of the lesson. So don't forget to acknowledge it—with gratitude."*

Neet turned to leave but before disappearing she threw one last remark over her shoulder. *"Oh, and take care of those bruises. Tomorrow might be worse."*

Rohil stood there fuming, watching her walk away. He shouted after her, *"I don't usually make mistakes, but choosing you as my trainer? That might have been a reckless misstep. But hey, better late than never, right? Tomorrow might just be the final straw—one step away from the last nail in the coffin. And if it is, well, you'll know exactly who gets the hit."*

Neet didn't turn back. Instead, she gave him an enigmatic look—one that unsettled Rohil more than he cared to admit. No matter how much he convinced himself otherwise, there was something about Neet he couldn't ignore. That uncertainty, that tug-of-war between admiration and frustration left him restless.

The next day in the gym Neet gripped an electronic knife, its blade sharp and pulsing with raw energy. Each touch sent strong volts crackling through the air and whenever it grazed Rohil's skin, a surge of agony shot through him—ten times worse than the sting of a stick. His gritted teeth barely contained his strangled cries as he dodged and weaved, desperate to stay out of her reach.

"Pain is just perception," Neet said, lunging forward again. *"The moment you change how you see it, it loses its power over you. Right now, you fear this knife because it's in my hands and as long as it stays with me, it can hurt you—wound you. In a real fight this blade could be deadly. It could even cost you your life. But if you push past that fear, act swiftly and endure the pain for just a moment to seize it from me, the threat disappears. And in that instant you'll discover something extraordinary—your endurance isn't just physical; it's a weapon inbuilt in you. So fight. Feel the pain. And understand its true nature."*

Rohil hesitated, but as Neet jabbed the knife into his side, something inside him shifted. Enough. Gritting his teeth, he ignored the pain, pushed forward, and grabbed Neet's wrist. Twisting her arm he threw her to the floor and pried the knife from her grasp. Gathering her composure, Neet took a deep breath and stood up, watching him with quiet approval.

Rohil tightened his grip around the knife, a smirk playing at the corner of his lips. *"Unbelievable... I didn't feel any pain from that last-minute, continuous jabbing of yours,"* he admitted with a hint of awe in his voice. He glanced at Neet, acknowledging her ingenious style of training.

"Keep practicing," Neet said simply, picking up her kit bag. Mysha clapped, followed by Unni and Komal.

Neet glanced at them all and said, *"This was the final chapter of your training. From here, it's up to you how you embrace and use it. I'll see you the day before the competition. Until then, all I can say is—good luck."*

She turned and left her footsteps fading into the distance. Yet even in her absence, her presence lingered. Rohil, piecing together every lesson she had drilled into them, finally understood the method behind her madness. But despite his growing admiration, he masked it with indifference. What troubled him most was that no matter how distant or dismissive he acted, Neet remained completely unaffected. And that more than anything unsettled him.

ENDURANCE TRAINING

Rohil's training was nothing short of brutal—a test of endurance, strength and willpower. He cycled through the untamed wilderness, his legs burning with each push of the pedals, sweat dripping down his face.

Back at the gym he gritted his teeth lifting heavy milk cans in both hands, his arms shaking under the strain. Mysha's stopwatch clicked—ten minutes. A milestone. His team erupted into applause their cheers fueling his determination.

The challenges only grew tougher. High on the monastery's ledge Rohil balanced upside down, his muscles trembling as he fought gravity. Below, Unni and Komal watched anxiously, gnawing at their nails, while Mysha timed his endurance. Meditation followed—silent, still, sharpening his mind, body and soul; forging a strength that couldn't be measured in muscle alone.

Pain was no longer an enemy to Rohil—it had become his closest companion. With each strike of the lama's staff against his shoulders, his muscles tensed but never wavered. The blows were fierce, a brutal test of his resilience, yet he stood firm, absorbing them like the mountains absorbed the howling winds. Each lash carved strength into his soul, forging him into something unbreakable. His body bore the bruises, but his mind remained untouched—an iron fortress against suffering.

In the gym, Rohil faced yet another trial—powerlifting, his body straining under the weight. Mysha, ever playful toyed with an electronic knife, letting its energy pulse against Rohil's skin. A slight twitch betrayed the shock but he didn't break focus. He completed his set, unfazed. Then with a smirk he turned on Mysha, ready to strike back. But before he could catch her she laughed, folded her hands in surrender and bent low handing over the knife—just as the lama had once done with the stick. Rohil paused, then smiled pulling her into a warm embrace.

Rahul's training was not for the faint-hearted. Day after day he pushed himself through the harshest elements, mastering the art of survival in the frozen wilderness.

With skis strapped to his feet he carved his way down treacherous slopes, his speed defying gravity, his instincts sharper than the biting wind. Each descent was a battle—dodging ice-laden obstacles, braving near-vertical drops and learning to trust the rhythm of the mountain beneath him.

On the jagged cliffs, he climbed with nothing but sheer willpower, his fingers clinging to icy rock faces, his muscles burning with effort. Every ledge, every crevice, every upward reach was a test of strength and precision. One wrong move and the depths would drag him under.

But the mountains had more trials to offer. Scaling walls of ice Rohil wielded his axes with precision, driving them into frozen sheets as he ascended into the unknown. The cold numbed his fingers, the wind roared its warnings but he climbed higher, defying both fear and fatigue.

And then there was the highline—a thin rope stretched between two towering cliffs, swaying with the wind, daring him to step forward. With arms outstretched for balance Rahul walked, each step a test of focus, each breath a silent war against gravity. Below him, the void yawned wide but his mind was unshaken.

This was more than training. This was preparation for something greater. The mountains would either break him—or forge him into something unstoppable.

The Frozen Himalayan Competition was not for the weak. It was a battle against nature, a test of sheer willpower. Rohil's training had been ruthless, sculpting him into the strongest contender for the title. But Abeer? Abeer had no intention of being left behind. His training every day was just as brutal, his resolve just as unshakable. If the mountain demanded more, he would give it everything.

High in the heart of the Himalayas where the air was thin and the peaks carved their way into the sky. Abeer stood before a sheer rock face. His body became one with the rock, each movement an act of trust, every muscle a thread in the delicate balance between triumph and a deadly fall.

But there was no time to rest. Training never stopped.

Dressed in nothing but a shorts, Abeer pedaled through snow-laden trails, his breath forming icy clouds in the freezing air. The cold gnawed at him, each gust of wind cutting through flesh like a blade but he pushed forward. The mountain would not break him.

Then came the river—a raging beast, wild and untamed. The water churned with merciless fury daring him to cross. Without hesitation, Abeer lifted his cycle onto his shoulders and stepped in. The icy current gripped him instantly, wrapping around his legs like shackles pulling, dragging and threatening to steal the very breath from his lungs. Every step was war, every movement an act of defiance against nature's fury. But he did not stop. He reached the other side drenched, shivering and barely able to feel his own limbs. And yet, without pause he climbed back onto his bike and rode on. The fire in his soul burning brighter than the frost on his skin.

Then came the stillness—a different kind of trial, but no less punishing.

Abeer stood at the edge of a cliff, the world stretching endlessly below him. Bare-chested against the biting wind he moved through the hardest yoga postures, his body twisting into near-impossible shapes, his breath steady despite the deadly drop just inches away. One slip, one slip-up, and the abyss would claim him. But fear had no place here. He moved with grace, with power; mastering his body, mastering his mind. Where others would see danger, Abeer found tranquility.

Blindfolded, Abeer launched himself down a treacherous slope, skiing at breakneck speed. There was no sight, no safety—only instinct. The wind howled, the snow rushed past, the earth tilted and shifted beneath him but he did not fall. He weaved through obstacles with precision, trusting something far beyond his senses.

This was more than training. This was transformation. The mountain was not his enemy—it was his forge. And when the Frozen Himalayan Competition began, Abeer would not just survive.

He would conquer. ---

The day had finally arrived for Rohil to confront the challenge that once humbled him—to climb the rock face blindfolded. It was the very test that had marked the beginning of his training with Neet, a trial that had once seemed insurmountable. Back then, he had hesitated, faltered and let doubt dictate his movements. But today was different. Every fall, every bruise, every lesson carved into his muscles and mind had led him to this moment. This was more than just a climb—it was proof of how far he had come. And this time, he wouldn't let fear stand in his way.

Today, Neet would decide whether he was ready—whether he was strong enough, skilled enough and fit enough to face the competition. If she deemed him unprepared there would be no second chances. No retries. It would mean the end of the road. He'd have to abandon the idea of competing altogether, pack his bags and return to the corporate life he had left behind. The thought sent a wave of unease through him, but there was no room for doubt now.

At the base of a towering rock face Rohil stood blindfolded, his fingers tracing the rough surface as he climbed. Neet moved alongside him, observing his every move with a sharp discerning eye. Below, Mysha, Unni, and Komal recorded the climb, their cameras capturing every slip, every struggle, and every triumph. Though Rohil faltered multiple times, he climbed with precision, adjusting swiftly to every misstep. The rock face was sheer, almost like a vertical wall and as it neared the summit, it narrowed dangerously. Finally, Rohil reached the top. His breath came in ragged gasps, his body aching but the thrill of accomplishment pulsed through him.

"Take off your blindfold," Neet instructed.

As he did, the vast openness around him sent a rush of adrenaline through his veins. He had done it. But Neet wasn't finished with him yet. She gestured ahead, where a perilously thin, uneven path—barely 30 centimeters wide—stretched like a frail bridge between their rock and another towering formation. On either side, the abyss plunged 2,000 meters into certain death.

Without hesitation, Neet stepped onto the path, her movements fluid and effortless. She crossed with perfect balance, climbing the towering rock formation on the other side before perching herself at its peak. From her elevated position she looked down at Rohil with an amused glint in her eyes.

Determined, Rohil prepared to follow. He took a step forward, but just as his foot hovered over the edge, Neet's voice cut through the wind.

"Blindfold yourself."

His heart skipped a beat. *"Are you serious?"*

Neet only smirked.

A flicker of doubt crept into him but Rohil wouldn't back down now. With a steadying breath, he tied the blindfold back over his eyes. Slowly, carefully, he moved forward, each step an act of blind trust.

"This path is a nightmare," he muttered.

"And what did you expect?" Neet grinned. "That someone would come pave it for you?"

"You could've at least warned me!" he shot back.

Neet chuckled. *"The fight is yours alone, Rohil. Get used to it."*

As Rohil inched forward, a sudden wave of apprehension washed over him. A nagging unease crept into his mind, prickling at his senses. Something felt off. His instincts flared, warning him to stop. He hesitated.

"Is there a gap ahead?" he asked. The silence stretched, thick and unyielding. Rohil waited, his breath shallow but Neet didn't answer.

Rohil exhaled sharply. *"If I keep relying on her, I'll be dead before I know it,"* he slurred to himself. *"Time to trust my own decisions."*

He tensed his muscles calculating the distance in his mind, then leaped. His hands found the rough surface of the rock tower on the other side, and he gripped it tightly pulling himself up. Hand over hand, he climbed until he reached the top. As he yanked off the blindfold, exhilaration surged through him. He had accomplished it.

Neet studied him for a moment then for the first time gave him a nod of approval. "Good job."

Before he could respond, she took a step back—and leaped off the towering rock face.

Rohil's stomach clenched as he watched her plunge into the open air. At the last moment she pulled the cord of her parachute and it unfurled above her, carrying her gracefully into the air.

His triumph turned to panic. *Hey!" he shouted after her. "And how exactly am I supposed to get down? I don't even have a parachute!*

But Neet only cackled, her figure growing smaller as the wind carried her away.

DESIRE VS. MORALS

The evening before the Frozen Himalayan Competition, the small Himalayan town pulsed with energy. Mall Road teemed with tourists and sports enthusiasts, while shops, hotels, and restaurants brimmed beyond capacity. Yet, in the camps of the contenders a stark contrast prevailed—tension hung thick in the air, mounting with each passing second. Rohil and his team were no exception. Inside his gym a heavy silence settled as Neet packed her bag, ready to leave after completing her assignment of training Rohil for the competition. With her role fulfilled she was prepared to move on, leaving Rohil and his team to forge their path forward alone.

Over the past month Neet had formed a close bond with Mysha, built on mutual admiration and respect. Now, as the moment of departure arrived Mysha struggled to find the right words. *"Keep in touch,"* she finally said, her voice laced with emotion.

Neet smiled, *"Of course."*

They embraced holding on for a second longer before Neet turned toward the door.

Her relationship with Rohil, however, was far from simple. Rohil wanted her on his team following his lead, his vision. But Neet, strong-willed and independent had always been clear—she made her own choices. This defiance unsettled Rohil.

"Everyone wants to be part of a winning team. Don't you?" he asked, arrogance lining his words.

Neet remained composed, her voice unwavering. *"My job was to train you, Rohil. Work can give me money and recognition but my character is shaped by my personal life. And my personal life is with Abeer."*

Rohil's jaw tightened. He hated her answer. As she turned to leave, he made one last attempt to sway her. *"We'll double your salary."*

Neet paused, then turned back, her gaze sharp with conviction. *"If money were everything, rich people wouldn't be donating theirs. The truth is, those with the most wealth are often the most insecure because they know that what's in their pockets today could be in someone else's tomorrow. In their desperation to hold onto it they lose their character. I'd rather live with less than compromise who I am."*

Agitated, Rohil scoffed. *"You and your boyfriend Abeer love giving lectures. Why not start delivering sermons? Might actually be a profitable business ."*

Neet ignored him and walked away, leaving Rohil fuming. Mysha, watching the exchange, stepped in. *"Let her go, Rohil,"* she said quietly.

His frustration only grew. *"She doesn't understand. We would value her more than Abeer ever could."*

Mysha shook her head. *"That's what you think, not her."*

Rohil's stubbornness flared. *"Then make her understand."*

Something in Mysha snapped. *"Not all of your wishes can come true."*

"They have to." Rohil's voice was firm, almost desperate.

Exasperated, Mysha shot him a sharp look. *"Go to hell."* As she walked away, she muttered, *"You're just stressed about the competition. Chill out a little."*

The strain of the upcoming event was beginning to show, manifesting in cracks within the team. Stress has a way of clouding judgment—it heightens emotions, distorts reality, and convinces people that their actions are unquestionably right. If only one person succumbs to it, others can still bring balance with logic and reason. But when an entire team gets caught in its grip, rational thinking fades, leaving no one to steady the ship.

Amidst the snow-covered peaks, beneath an evening sky painted in hues of twilight, Neet curled up in Abeer's arms by the flickering bonfire. The warmth of the flames cast a golden glow on their faces, contrasting against the biting cold that surrounded them. Their tent stood close by swaying gently with the mountain breeze, as soft music played in the background—an almost surreal setting; perfect for a stolen moment of love before the storm of competition. The Frozen Himalayan challenge awaited them at dawn but for now, Neet allowed herself to melt into Abeer's embrace cherishing the rare stillness.

"There's nothing in this world better than hugging you," she murmured, her voice barely above a whisper.

Abeer smiled, though his thoughts were elsewhere. For once, the man who always listened to his heart was lost in strategy. The competition loomed over him, demanding his attention even in this intimate moment.

"How was your training with Rohil?" he asked casually, but Neet wasn't fooled. She could sense the unspoken curiosity, the underlying need to know more—not just about her training, but about Rohil himself. Whether Abeer admitted it or not he wanted to gauge his rival's progress.

Neet smirked, a teasing glint in her eyes. *"I'm in such a romantic mood, and you're asking about Rohil's training? Why don't you just go have an affair with him?"*

Abeer let out a low chuckle, shaking his head. *"There are always two kind of people who stay close to you—one is your love interest, and the other is your hate interest."* He minced his words, realizing he had revealed more of his true feelings than he intended. *"I mean, your opponent."*

Neet laughed, but she didn't let the conversation drift away.

"You're right, though. If there's anyone who could challenge you in the competition, it's Rohil. He's exceptional. No matter who trained him, he would have always reached the same level." She paused before tilting her head curiously. *"But why did you ask me to train him in the first place?"*

For a moment, the flickering flames reflected in Abeer's eyes, his expression hardening with quiet confidence. It was rare to see this side of him—the fierce competitor who hid beneath his usual restrained demeanor.

"I didn't want him to have any excuses if he lost to me in the competition," he admitted, his voice edged with certainty. *"I leveled the playing field so that when he falls, there's no room for doubt—no excuses, no debates, just the undeniable truth of who the real champion is. Now, finally, we stand as equals for the ultimate face-off."* Abeer hissed, his anger crackling like a live wire.

Neet studied him, intrigued. *"But isn't that a disadvantage for you? You trained your own competition. Won't that work against you?"*

Abeer's gaze didn't waver. *"Can raw iron ore ever become strong without first enduring the searing heat of the furnace? Likewise, a true champion must withstand fierce competition—only then can victory be truly earned. Just as darkness gives meaning to light, triumph only holds value when there is defeat. Without opposites, nothing can stand on its own. There is no glory in standing on the podium with a gold medal if there is no second place. Champions are forged in battle, tested by adversity, and defined by their greatest rivals—and I need Rohil for that."*

Neet frowned slightly, mulling over his words. *"Isn't it all about winning and losing in competition? Why does an opponent matter to you?"*

"Some athletes play for the sheer thrill of the sport, unburdened by victory or defeat. Their rush comes not from winning, but from the skis slicing through snow, the wind roaring past. But true competition demands more—a force that turns passion into the will to win. Without it, the fight feels empty. For me, that force is Rohil."

Neet listened, astonished by Abeer's fervor. *"So, you knew Rohil would take the challenge and fight in the Frozen Himalayan Competition?"* she asked, her curiosity piqued.

Abeer's lips curled into a knowing smirk. *"I was certain. That's why I challenged him right there, in the middle of the office, in front of everyone."*

His words carried the weight of intent, a battle already unfolding in his mind. Neet suddenly grasped the deeper meaning behind his actions. This wasn't just about the competition—it was about proving something far beyond the sport itself. She grew interested; she wanted to delve into the depths of Abeer's mind.

"Hence you wanted this showdown, to settle the score with Rohil, didn't you?" She murmured, piecing it all together.

Abeer's gaze drifted toward the towering peaks. their icy summits gleaming under the stars filled sky. *"I didn't just want this—I needed it."* At that moment, Abeer paused, lost in contemplation. *"My father raised me on benevolence, but in sports, kindness doesn't win. If I follow his path, I may never claim victory. Rohil is my spark—his presence pushes me beyond my limits, driving me toward the Frozen Himalayan title. Without him, I'd be content playing simply for the love of the sport. Yet, victory isn't my ultimate goal in this competition. It's merely a means— to prove to my mother that my father was the real hero. And to show the world that an athlete's worth isn't measured by conquest alone. Sometimes, the greatest triumph is staying true to the craft, playing not for the world, but for oneself."*

Neet inhaled sharply, The Frozen Himalayan Competition wasn't just another game for Abeer, it was the ultimate reckoning. Abeer leaned in, his voice unwavering. *"That being said, winning and losing are just how a game ends. If you truly want to grow as a sports person, you must support your opponent—because they're the ones who push you to give your best. That's the real victory in the competitive world. Either stay out of the competition, or if you decide to step in, give it everything you've got."*

Neet narrowed her eyes playfully. *"And what if, after all this, you still lose in the end?"*

Abeer paused before answering Neet. This response of Abeer is what defines him—not just as a competitor, but as a person. Despite his drive to reach the top, demanded by the moment, he has the maturity to see the bigger picture—the picture of life.

"Then that too is a victory," Abeer replied without hesitation. *"A true winner isn't defined by a single triumph or loss, but by their potential. Wins and losses can be manipulated, but real talent speaks for itself. If, after all this, defeat still comes my way, I'll accept it with grace and work even harder for the next time. Life is a cycle—it keeps moving, no matter what."*

Neet let out a short laugh, shaking her head. *"Here we go again with the existential outlook. You're even crazier than Rohil."*

Abeer smirked. *"That's exactly why I gave him my best trainer."*

Neet leaned in closer, her posture softening with a touch of longing. Her lips brushing against his with a playful glimmer in her eyes. *"I happen to be the best in many things."*

Abeer raised an eyebrow, intrigued. *"Like what? Please, elaborate."*

With a soft touch, she traced her fingers across his forehead, her voice dropping to a whisper. *"I'm good at immersing you in love and taking away all your stress and worries."*

Abeer exhaled a slow smile, pulling her into a deep embrace, his lips finding hers once again. The cold of the Himalayan night didn't stand a chance against the fire between them.

CHAPTER - 6

FROZEN RIVALRY

The narrative of the book 'Fitrat' comes full circle as the story returns to the Frozen Himalayan Competition 2023. Here, Abeer and Rohil collide, shaping an explosive and uncertain future.

As a quick recap, Rohil had just lost the very first ski jump match to Abeer—by a mere two centimeters. The difference was minuscule but to him it felt like a landslide. His chest heaved, fists clenched at his sides. Losing was never an option, and now, faced with an unexpected defeat—especially to Abeer—his frustration spiraled into raw fury.

Rohil ripped off his gear and flung it to the ground, the crunch of snow beneath his boots doing little to soften the violence in his movements. Mysha stepped forward cautiously, her voice calm yet firm.

"It's okay, Rohil. This was just the first match—we still have a long road ahead."

But it wasn't. Not to him. The words barely registered as his anger boiled over. His body moved before his mind could stop it—he shoved Mysha aside, as though she were just another hurdle in his path. He panted for air, his face flushed as he shouted,

"A loss is a loss! It can never be okay!"

The crowd fell into a stunned silence. Mysha staggered but caught herself quickly. The humiliation of being pushed in front of everyone burned through her shock, replacing it with defiance. Without hesitation, she stepped up and shoved him back, her voice sharp with warning.

"Control your anger, Rohil. Or it won't end well—not for our relationship, and certainly not for your competition."

Mysha turned on her heel and strode away, leaving Rohil standing in the snow, his fury simmering in the cold air.

That night at Rohil's team residence the air was thick with tension, a silence stretching through every corner of the house. In the dimly lit living room Mysha sat with a glass of drink, her fingers absently tracing the rim as her mind wrestled with the evening's events—Rohil's reaction, his anger, his refusal to accept what had happened. He stood by the window his posture rigid, his breath uneven. The weight of failure clung to him like an unbearable shadow. And then, as if the frustration inside him became too much to contain, he lashed out. His fist slammed against the windowpane.

The sharp sound of shattering glass broke the silence. Shards scattered onto the floor and crimson streaks bloomed across his knuckles. Blood dripped slowly but he didn't flinch. He just stood there staring at the broken glass as if it mirrored something inside him.

Unni, who had been quietly nursing his drink, sighed and leaned back.

"Rohil, acting like this will only hurt you. Consider this loss an experience. Accept it and move forward." He said

Rohil turned sharply, his eyes dark with fury and strode toward him.

"I didn't come here to accept defeat. I'm used to experiencing nothing but victory."

Mysha exhaled sharply, setting down her glass with a little too much force. She had been patient but now her patience was slipping.

"Then what happened today? If losing is such a big problem for you, why didn't you perform? The mistake was yours, yet you're taking it out on us. We're here to support you, not to be humiliated." Mysha's tone was laced with bitterness.

For a moment, Rohil's grip on his anger wavered. The throbbing pain in his hand, the warmth of his own blood—it was grounding him, pulling him out of his storm of rage. His expression flickered, something bitter twisting at his lips. *"Amazing. Even luck was on Abeer's side today."* He muttered.

Mysha didn't hold back and commented, *"Then you should have beaten luck too."*

Her words cut deeper than she realized. A shadow passed over Rohil's face, his jaw tightening as his mind drifted to a memory he had buried deep. His voice, when he finally spoke was different—lower, raw.

"The last time I lost, I was eighteen. I lost to my own father when he refused to invest in my app. He told me to earn my own money to build my startup from scratch. That day I realized something—if my own father was pushing me towards failure, no one else would ever give me a chance. I made a promise to myself that day. I swore I would never lose again. And today Abeer broke that promise. I couldn't prove myself to my father but I will prove to Abeer—and to everyone—that I am better than them."

A quiet understanding settled over the room. Mysha, Unni, and Komal exchanged glances, their frustration melting into something softer. They had been angry with him, disappointed even but now they saw the deeper wound he had been carrying. It wasn't just this loss—it was years of resentment of unhealed scars.

With quiet reassurance, Komal spoke, her voice filled with empathy. *"Rohil, there are still three more matches. I think we should focus on them."*

For the first time that night Rohil didn't lash out. He didn't argue. Instead, he crouched down and began picking up the shattered glass, his movements slow, thoughtful. As he cleaned the mess he had made, something in him seemed to shift as though he was piecing himself back together alongside the fragments.

Sensing the change, the others silently chose to give him space. One by one, they left the room—Mysha first, followed by Unni and Komal—leaving Rohil alone with his thoughts.

Abeer had always believed in gratitude. It wasn't just a habit but a way of life, something he had inherited from his father—a man of principle and humility. That gratitude extended to every challenge he faced and today standing before the towering snow-clad mountain, he felt it more than ever. The event hadn't even begun but he had arrived early, long before anyone else. In the silence of the morning with only the biting wind for company, he let himself absorb the presence of the mountain. It wasn't just an opponent to be conquered; it was a force to be understood, respected. He traced its form with his eyes mapping out ridges and slopes, gauging where the snow was soft enough to betray him and where it was solid enough to hold his weight. He knew better than to rush. A climb wasn't just about strength—it was about patience, about reading the mountain like a story written in ice and rock.

The crisp air carried the sound of footsteps behind him. Neet always arrived like a breeze, light and full of warmth carrying a presence that made everything feel a little easier. Holding up a small container, she grinned. *"If you're done whispering sweet nothings to the mountain, how about breakfast? It's still warm."*

Abeer smiled, shaking his head at her remark. *"A few more minutes. You go ahead, I'll join you soon."*

For a moment, their eyes met, and in that glance, there was a quiet understanding—one that needed no words. Neet settled on a rock nearby and Abeer turned back to his task.

Lifting his axe he tested the surface, striking in small deliberate motions. The snow was unpredictable—some areas gave way too easily crumbling under the lightest touch, while others were frozen solid, impenetrable. Finding the right place to start was crucial. His hands worked methodically feeling for the perfect spot, until—A sharp crunch of boots against ice pulled his focus away. It's Rohil.

Abeer didn't have to turn to know who it was. Rohil's presence carried a weight, an intensity that never failed to disrupt the air around them. Yesterday's ski-jumping event had ended in Abeer's victory, but the tension between them was far from settled. Rohil lingered for a moment then let out a small smirk.

"Not bad," he said. *"That win yesterday. Guess you had luck on your side."*

Abeer met his gaze, his expression steady. *"Thanks. Good luck for today's match."*

Rohil's smirk deepened. *"You'll need it more than I do. I used none of mine yesterday. Today, it's just me, my hard work and this mountain."* Rohil pointed toward the mountain with a gaze full of vengeance, as if it were a rival he was destined to conquer.

Every conversation between them carried an edge, sharp and deliberate, as if rivalry had become a language of its own. Abeer tilted his head slightly, amusement flickering in his eyes. *"Perhaps you should first master the art of respecting the mountains before attempting to climb them. Better yet, seek its permission before leaving your first footprint on its slopes. Believe it or not, doing so might just elevate your performance."*

Rohil let out a quiet chuckle, his gaze flicking toward the towering peak. *"Unlike you, I don't bow to them with reverence. I don't believe in that kind of corruption. Mountains exist to be conquered, and that's exactly what I do."*

With that razor-sharp remark Rohil cast one last glance at Abeer before turning on his heel and striding away, leaving Abeer with the remnants of his words. But Abeer had no time for distractions. He turned his attention back to the mountain, exhaling slowly. The real challenge was about to begin.

Even before the sun had a chance to spread its warmth across the slopes, the venue was already teeming with spectators, their excitement humming in the crisp morning air. The snow-covered mountains loomed majestically. The passionate mountaineering enthusiasts had gathered from around the world to witness the Frozen Himalayan Competition's second event—snow climbing.

"Welcome to the second event of the Frozen Himalayan Competition—snow climbing!" the commentator's voice rang through the loudspeakers, thick with anticipation. *"Water is an element of life, but today, it has become a harbinger of danger.The melting snow isn't just slippery; it's a silent predator waiting to strike."*

For the climbers, the soft trickle of melting snow was an ominous warning. It meant danger. The deadly mix of water and ice would make their ascent even more treacherous—slippery, slow, and unpredictable.

As the buzzer blared the competitors launched themselves forward, their bodies tensed with determination. At the forefront, Rohil moved with impressive agility, his confidence matched by his swift and decisive actions. Every step, every movement was sharp and precise, as if he had memorized the mountain's surface. But not far behind, Abeer climbed with resolute focus—steady, deliberate, his every action calculated to perfection. Meanwhile, others struggled against the elements. The loose snow, trickling water, the unexpected shifts in ice and the harsh conditions slowed them down, and some even lost their grip tumbling down before they could make it halfway.

Just before reaching the peak, Rohil hit a large patch of unstable snow. With every strike of his ice axe, chunks of it crumbled around him crashing down in heavy sheets. He struggled to secure his ice screws but they refused to hold. Frustration burned in his chest as he watched Abeer gaining on him. Desperation took over. He struck harder, hoping brute force would do what patience had failed to achieve. But the reckless movements only made things worse. The snow beneath him weakened, making his footing even more uncertain.

Abeer, on the other hand, remained focused. He maneuvered past the obstacles with calculated ease, overtaking Rohil just as they neared the summit. And then in a moment of quiet triumph, he reached the top first. Victory was his—again.

The crowd erupted in cheers as Abeer pulled himself up, victorious. Neet, unable to contain herself ran toward him throwing her arms around him in an embrace. Laughing softly, Abeer took her hand their fingers intertwining as they walked away together, their connection unspoken but undeniable.

Rohil, still at his spot was rigid with frustration. His jaw clenched, his fists tightening. And then, with a sharp exhale he lashed out—kicking at the snow, sending it flying in all directions.

"This competition just took an unexpected turn!" the commentator's voice boomed again. *"After today's match, no one can afford to underestimate India's position in this event. What Abeer has done in the last two rounds is nothing short of remarkable. At times, it felt like this entire competition was only between Abeer and Rohil!"*

But Rohil had already stopped listening. Without a word he turned away and started walking. The hotel was far but he didn't care. He needed the distance. Mysha hurried after him trying to speak but he brushed past her pushing her aside without so much as a glance, his frustration far too consuming to acknowledge anything else.

The night hung heavy over Rohil's shoulders pressing down like an invisible weight. He sat slouched in his dimly lit room, the amber glow of the bedside lamp barely reaching the dark corners. His first defeat had been hard enough to accept but the second—the one that stripped him of his pride and left him staring at his own shortcomings—was unbearable. He couldn't understand it, couldn't process how he had lost not once but twice. The bitterness sat thick in his chest, swirling like the drink in his glass. One drink turned into two then three, until logic and restraint bled away leaving behind only frustration and fire.

No one on his team dared approach him. They knew better. Rohil in defeat was a storm best avoided. But Mysha had always been different. She had been the one to ground him, to remind him of who he was beyond the competition. Yet tonight, even she seemed drained. Defeat had revealed something raw and unpleasant between them, something neither had been prepared to face.

A knock at his door barely registered over the haze in his mind. Unni stood there, hesitating before delivering the words that sent Rohil surging to his feet.

"Mysha is leaving."

The glass in his hand slammed onto the table, the liquid sloshing over the sides. His pulse pounded, his anger reigniting. Without a second thought he stormed down the hallway, his footsteps unsteady but determined.

He burst into Mysha's room like a storm, the door swinging open with force. She turned, startled but unsurprised. They had known each other for years, had built something strong—or so she had thought. But now under the weight of back-to-back losses she saw a version of Rohil she hadn't known existed. The real test of a person's character wasn't in their victories but in how they handled defeat. And the man standing before her, eyes clouded with fury and alcohol was a stranger.

"You can't just walk away like this!" Rohil's voice was sharp, accusing.

Mysha met his gaze, unflinching. *"I'm not her to serve you, Rohil."* Her voice didn't waver, but there was an edge to it—one that hadn't been there before. *"My mother used to say that if you want to see someone's true nature, watch how they behave when they lose. And I have to say, the version of you that loses is absolutely disgusting."*

Her words struck like ice but Rohil was too far gone to hear the truth in them. Instead, he lashed out, his pride refusing to back down.

"And I see a traitor in you," he shot back, his tone venomous. *"I don't need people who betray me—not in this competition, not in my life."*

A flicker of hurt crossed Mysha's face but she refused to let it break her. *"Correct yourself, Rohil,"* she said, her voice quieter now but no less firm. *"I didn't come here for the competition. I came here for us. For our love"*

Rohil let out a bitter laugh, shaking his head. *"Love? What love? The kind that disappears the moment things get difficult?"*

Tears threatened to spill from Mysha's eyes but she held them back. Instead, she let out a small humorless chuckle, shaking her head as if finally understanding something. *"I thought you came to stop me from leaving,"* she whispered. *"But instead, you came to tell me that you're the one who is throwing me out. Impressive. Your ego is truly unmatched, Rohil. Today, you didn't just lose to Abeer—you lost me too."*

The tension in the room was suffocating. Rohil's grip tightened, and in a burst of rage, he grabbed the glass from the table and hurled it at the floor. It shattered into countless shards, scattering between them like the remains of something irreparable.

Mysha flinched at the sound but didn't turn back. She had nothing left to say. As the first tear finally slipped down her cheek, she walked past him, leaving Rohil standing in the wreckage of his own making.

The diner in the town was a haven against the freezing cold outside. The snow fell in thick solemn flakes, mirroring the dejection in Rohil's heart as he stepped inside. He carried the weight of defeat on his shoulders.

At the counter Abeer sat with Neet, their laughter low and effortless, their glasses half-full. The sight of them made Rohil's chest tighten. His gaze met Abeer's across the room and for a moment neither looked away.

Rohil turned, grabbed a drink and sank into a secluded corner, away from them. He wanted solitude. Instead, he got Abeer.

Without a word, Abeer slid onto the stool beside him. They drank in silence, the warmth of their drink dulling the sting of the night. For a while, neither of them spoke—two climbers, two competitors, lost in their own thoughts. Then, finally Rohil exhaled and broke the silence.

"Congratulations once again," he said, the words laced with something unreadable. *"You're just inches away from winning the competition."*

Abeer didn't smirk. He didn't boast. There was no trace of arrogance on his face—only a quiet, unshaken calm, as if he himself had undergone a metamorphosis. To him, victory was no longer a pedestal to stand on; it was just a fleeting, fragile moment. Rohil hadn't expected that.

"Winning isn't about defeating your opponent," Abeer said simply, his voice steady. *"If you've given your game your full effort—with honesty and dedication—then you're already a winner. First place, second place… those are just numbers. My father always used to tell me this, but as I grew up, I lost his pearls of wisdom in the fog of my ego. And now, when I am so close to winning, it suddenly feels meaningless."* Abeer, naturally introspective, found himself lost in thought as he poured his heart out to Rohil.

Rohil let out a short, bitter laugh. *"That's easy to say when you're sitting at the top. But let's not fool ourselves. Whether you play fair or not, it doesn't matter. If you win, you're number one."*

Abeer shook his head slightly, as if he had heard this argument a thousand times before. He wasn't irritated. He wasn't surprised. To the world, winning was everything. Integrity was secondary. But Abeer didn't care about how the world perceived things. His principles were unshaken.

"You can win by cheating, by manipulation, by bending the rules," Abeer said, his voice steady. *"And maybe no one will ever know. But you will. At the end of the day you have to answer to yourself. How do you justify a victory when deep inside, you know someone else deserved it more?"*

Something in Rohil shifted. The words struck him deeper than he wanted to admit. He had grown up believing that in the game of life, deception and manipulation were fair play. But now, as he sat there worn out and defeated, he realized there was truth in Abeer's words.

Under any other circumstance he would have fought back, argued, torn Abeer's philosophy apart. But tonight he was too tired to deny the truth. And perhaps, for the first time, he was willing to listen.

Abeer leaned forward slightly, his voice quiet but firm. *"You want to defeat me, Rohil. That's why you climb—to conquer. But the mountain doesn't understand victory or defeat. When you drive a screw into the rock, it grips tighter, making itself stronger so you don't fall. If you respect the mountain, it will show you the path to the summit on its own. Climb for the sheer joy of it, without thinking about me. What follows will be a true testament to your effort. The fulfillment of giving your all and embracing the journey will always be more rewarding than any gold medal."*

Abeer stood up, setting his glass down with a soft thud. Before walking away, he turned one last time.

"Tomorrow, the climber in me will rise to the challenge again with everything I have. Come prepared. Wishing you the best."

And just like that, Abeer was gone.

Rohil sat there, staring at his drink. Slowly, he dipped a finger into the liquid and stirred, watching the ripples spread across the surface. His thoughts churned the same way, unraveling, reforming, reshaping everything he had once believed.

For the first time in his life, he wasn't thinking about winning.

He was thinking about *what winning truly meant.*

In the hush of the early morning, Rohil woke to the fierce howling of the wind. Rising from his bed he unlatched the window, only to be met by a violent gust of rain that lashed against his face. The cold stung his skin forcing him to slam the window shut. He stood still for a moment, his chest rising and falling with quiet determination. Without hesitation he grabbed his kit bag, slung it over his shoulder and walked out into the storm.

The rock climbing venue loomed in the distance shrouded in mist and rain. The sky was still a deep shade of blue, the first hints of dawn breaking through the heavy clouds. Rohil ran through the downpour, his footsteps echoing in the empty terrain. For the first time he was alone— no teammates, no familiar voices to push him forward. When he finally reached the rock face, he came to a halt breathless and drenched. Slowly, he reached out and placed his hand against the cold wet stone feeling the pulse of something greater than himself. A deep emotion stirred within him as he knelt down, his fingers tracing the rugged surface. His eyes turned misty as he lifted his gaze looking at the rock not as an obstacle but with reverence.

A presence approached. Abeer had arrived, his sharp eyes taking in the scene before him. A small smile played at the corner of his lips as he watched Rohil. Their eyes met briefly an unspoken exchange passing between them. Then without a word Abeer turned his attention to the rock, mapping its surface, studying its treacherous edges and preparing his mind for the climb ahead.

The commentator's voice echoed through the rain, crackling through the speakers.

"The incessant downpour has transformed the rock climbing event into an even greater test of skill and endurance. And with today's match being a decisive one, the stakes couldn't be higher. Abeer, already leading the points tally with two points, stands on the verge of securing an unassailable lead. A victory here would add another point to Abeer's kitty, making the final match a mere formality, as the last event offers only two points—insufficient to even match Abeer's score. More than just a personal triumph, his win would mark a historic moment for India—never before in the history of the Frozen Himalayan Competition has an Indian claimed the title. Today, Abeer has the chance to etch his name into the annals of the sport."

The third event began. The rain had turned the rock into a merciless opponent, slick and treacherous. Bruno Botta surged ahead his movements fueled by a thirst for dominance. Below him, Abeer struggled against the slimy surface his footing unstable. Rohil, too fought to find his grip. Frustration gnawed at him until, suddenly, his eyes caught sight of a thin crack running up the rock's surface. It was almost imperceptible—a narrow path hidden in the chaos. Awe flickered in his gaze but he wasted no time. With swift precision he secured his grip, driving nuts into the crack and pulling himself upward with newfound speed.

As he reached Botta's level, a disturbing sight made his jaw tighten. Botta was deliberately dislodging rocks, sending them tumbling down onto Abeer. The sharp fragments struck Abeer's helmet, disrupting his rhythm and slowing him down. Rohil's eyes narrowed. His gaze locked onto Botta's and in a single calculated move he surged past him. Once above, he let loose a cascade of debris, letting gravity deliver his message.

"What the hell do you think you're doing?" Botta snarled, anger flashing in his eyes.

Rohil's voice was steady, unwavering. *"Every action has an equal and opposite reaction. These are the consequences of your own actions and now you have to bear them. In my country, Bruno is a name given to dogs and I don't waste my breath arguing with them. Jusy play your game right."*

Botta seethed, determined to catch up and make Rohil pay for his derogatory remarks. But in his haste to climb up, he miscalculated. His foot slipped, his grip failed and he plummeted down to a lower point on the rock face.

Rohil pushed forward, inching closer to the peak when a formidable overhanging curve loomed in his path, blocking his ascent. Without a moment's hesitation he executed a daring back-hang maneuver, suspending himself upside down from the rock's underside. His body hung precariously, his hands hovering in empty space while only his legs remained hooked to the underside's jagged edge. Thousands of feet below, the abyss yawned, unforgiving and absolute.

With a powerful burst of motion, he swung his body upward. For a fleeting second, he was weightless—no grip, no anchor, nothing but sheer trust in his own strength. At the perfect moment, he grasped the hinge point on the outer curve with unwavering precision. As his grip tightened, securing his hold, he released his legs from their precarious position and surged over the daunting ledge, reclaiming control of the climb. From there, the rest of the climb was no longer a battle—it was his victory to claim.

He reached the summit first. His competitors were still far below, battling against the merciless rock. Moments later, Abeer pulled himself up onto the peak.

At the outset Rohil did not celebrate. No victorious outcry, no raised fists. Instead, he turned to Abeer. Their eyes met and a small knowing smirk crossed Abeer's face—a silent acknowledgment of defeat. He gave a slight nod. Rohil returned the gesture. No words were needed. Without another glance they both turned and walked their separate ways.

After his triumphant victory in the rock-climbing match, Rohil felt something shift within him. It wasn't the usual high of winning, the fleeting rush of adrenaline that demanded the world's applause. No, this time the victory felt different—quieter, deeper. It was a win not over an opponent but over himself. And there was only one place he wanted to be right now.

He found Mysha in her room, suitcase packed, ready to leave. The sight of her standing there on the verge of walking away from him, sent a sharp jolt through his chest. Without thinking he stepped in, blocking her path. Never before he allowed himself to be vulnerable.

"*I'm sorry.*" His voice was raw, stripped of ego, stripped of pride.

Mysha's fingers tightened around the suitcase handle. Unaware of the day's events and the transformation Rohil had undergone, Mysha was still holding onto the discord between them. As far as she was concerned, the rift between them was beyond repair.

"There's nothing left between us, Rohil. So what difference does an apology make?" Mysha voice was cold.

She turned to leave but he followed her, his words spilling out faster than he could control.

"It took me time to understand, Mysha. I wasn't angry at my father—I was angry at myself. Because no matter how hard I tried, I never felt like I was worth anything. So, every time I saw competition, I threw myself into it like a reckless fool, thinking that if I won, maybe— just maybe—I would prove my worth. But I was wrong." His voice wavered, his usual bravado peeling away to reveal something real, something raw. In that unprecedented moment, he acknowledged his flaws, his fears, and most of all, his gratitude toward Mysha.

"Thank you. You've done so much for me," he continued, his tone thick with emotion. *"And yet, like an ungrateful sucker, I kept demanding more—never stopping to think about what I had done for you in return."*

Tears pricked at Mysha's eyes. She had never imagined that Rohil would ever change, had never demanded anything from him, only accepted him as he was. The distance between them had never been built on hatred—it had been the result of situations, of stress, of competition pulling them apart when all they wanted was to hold on. And now, seeing him like this standing before her, admitting his mistakes with an honesty she never thought possible, she realized how pointless it was to keep holding onto her grudges.

But instead of drowning the moment in heavy emotions, Mysha took a lighthearted approach to smooth out the creases in their relationship.

"So, what do I do now? Stay back? But only if you promise to help me unpack my bags," she teased, her lips curving into a small smile.

Rohil let out a breath he hadn't realized he was holding and nodded. She pulled him into a tight embrace, melting away the last remnants of their fight.

"One thing's for sure," Rohil said, smirking. *"You don't put up much of a fight."*

She arched a brow, mischief twinkling in her tear-brimmed eyes.

"You don't argue with a stubborn, emotionally unsettled child. You just smother them with love until they come back to their senses."

A chuckle escaped his lips before she kissed him, sealing the moment with something far stronger than words. The storm had passed. And just like that, they had found their way back to each other.

Lost in the depth of their emotions, Mysha and Rohil clung to each other, their make-up kiss stretching far beyond reason. Neither wanted to break away, bound by an unspoken promise, wrapped in the warmth of their love. Time, for them had ceased to exist—until reality came rushing back. Mysha's eyes fluttered open as a sudden realization struck her. Evening had already settled in, casting a golden hue over the horizon. The pre-final customary ritual of the Frozen Himalayan Competition awaited them. She pulled away breathless as the weight of the moment sank in. Rohil exhaled sharply coming to the same realization.

This was no ordinary ritual. Locals believed it to be a sacred rite—one that cleansed the spirit, warding off negativity while infusing the contenders with strength and resilience. And they would need every ounce of it. The final leg of the competition was known to be brutal, a battle against nature itself where survival was not guaranteed. It was here, on this last stretch that most challengers succumbed, lost to the merciless terrain of the frozen Himalayas.

Later, in her room Mysha stood before the mirror draping herself in an elegant ethnic dress, the fabric flowing like whispers of the wind. The ritual demanded tradition and she honored it. Just as she secured the last pin in place the quiet creak of the door made her pause. She didn't need to turn—she already knew. Rohil was here.

A small smile tugged at her lips as she met his gaze through the reflection. *"Now that you've found this newfound wisdom, this quiet restraint, does that mean you won't fight for things anymore? Because, you know… with this mindset, complacency can creep in before you realize it."*

For a moment silence hung between them. Then, something shifted in Rohil. His posture straightened, a familiar glint returning to his eyes—not the reckless fire of before but something different. A controlled storm. A tempered force. It reminded her of Abeer's way of thinking—calculated, yet unshakable.

"What are you saying?" Rohil scoffed, stepping forward. *"Of course, I will fight. And I will win everytime. But I will change the way I play my game."*

Mysha turned to face him fully now, searching his face. A wave of fear and insecurity seeped into Mysha. *"Change is happening so fast, Rohil. What if, in trying to evolve, you lose the old version of yourself? What if you become someone who belongs neither here nor there?"*

A quiet chuckle escaped him as he leaned against the doorframe.

"You're overthinking it, Mysha. Emotions aren't meant to be sorted like numbers on a spreadsheet. You'll never balance them perfectly. They're fleeting, shifting with the tides of life. I've realized that clinging to an old mindset is doing me more harm than good. That means it's time to adapt. Right now, the best version of me is one who fights with controlled aggression."

Mysha watched him for a long moment, her heart thrumming with something she couldn't quite name. Then, a slow smile spread across her lips. *"I won't lie… this new you is difficult to grasp. But you know what? I think I love him even more."*

Rohil grinned, reaching for her hand, his grip firm yet gentle.

"That's all I needed to hear. Your approval seals the deal."

With that, he pulled her along, stepping out into the night, ready to embrace whatever lay ahead. Mysha followed, stealing a glance at him, her heart swelling with something fierce and unbreakable.

The snow-laden valley glowed under the flickering light of a hundred butter lamps, their flames dancing like tiny stars against the vast frozen expanse. Towering mountain peaks stood solemnly in the background, their icy crowns kissed by the evening light. The air was thick with the scent of burning incense as smoke spiraled into the sky from the ritual fire. Monks, lamas, and sages sat in deep concentration, their chants rising and falling like waves, carrying ancient prayers into the wind. The rhythmic beat of drums, the soft chime of bells and the deep resonant hum of long trumpets filled the valley, weaving a hypnotic spell over the gathered crowd. It was a ritual of strength meant to cleanse the spirits of the competitors and prepare them for the trials ahead. As the final prayers were uttered, ashes from the sacred fire were cast into the sky, dissolving into the night like fleeting wishes.

As the ceremony came to an end, the atmosphere shifted. The sacred moment was replaced with murmurs of excitement and congratulatory handshakes, all directed toward Rohil who had just secured a major victory in the last event. The competitors and their teams gathered around him, some in admiration, others already strategizing for the next battle. Amid the sea of voices, a familiar one cut through the noise.

"Congratulations." Abeer said, extending a hand.

Rohil turned to see Abeer standing before him, hand extended. Something about the way he said it—calm, measured—sent a ripple through Rohil's competitive instincts. His usual cocky smirk surfaced as he grasped Abeer's hand. *"Thanks. That speech of yours was pretty remarkable. I took all the best parts, applied them to my game and ended up beating you. You really shouldn't have shared your secrets. Well! You've only made things harder for yourself."*

Abeer chuckled, unfazed. *"Neet had already trained you well, but even then, you couldn't break through to victory. After losing to me twice in a row, I started thinking—maybe you weren't quite at my level yet. You needed something more. A push. A shift in perspective. That's what I gave you. Your last win only proves one thing—we are finally equals now."* He paused, his eyes gleaming with a quiet intensity before adding, *"But don't mistake this for generosity. I did it for myself. I needed to bring you up to my level so that I could defeat you at your best. I want the world to see, once and for all, who the true champion is."*

Rohil's smirk widened, his blood thrumming with adrenaline.

"Oh! Now I see—you shift between two extremes like a chameleon of thought. One moment, you're a sage, untouched by worldly desires, floating beyond notions of winning and losing. The next, you're a sharp-witted strategist, ruthless and cunning, playing only to win. Is it fair to say you dance between wisdom and war?"

Abeer leans in, his gaze intense, as if unveiling a hidden layer of his soul—a secret only a chosen few are meant to hear.

"It all depends on time and circumstance. Last night called for wisdom, so I became the sage, preaching detachment and higher truths. But now, the battlefield demands a warrior, and here I stand, sharp and ruthless, throwing down a challenge. I walk the fine line between enlightenment and conquest—balancing wisdom with war."

Rohil, a master of deception in his own right, fires back with a razor-sharp retort, a comeback so precise it lands like a well-aimed punch.

"I have to admit, you played a clever game. But let me tell you something—the finals? That's mine. Just watch how I turn the tables."

Abeer's lips curled into a knowing smile. *"All the best, then."*

"To you as well." Rohil responded, his voice dripping with sarcasm.

Consequently, they parted ways, their footsteps leaving deep imprints in the snow. Neither looked back, their minds already locked on the final battle ahead. The hunger for victory burned between them, fierce and undeniable. Knowing that only one of them would walk away as the true champion.

THE FINAL SHOWDOWN

The air was razor-sharp with cold, the kind that bit through layers of gear and scraped against bare skin like shards of ice. The **Marathon Climb**—the final and most brutal challenge of the competition—was set against the towering peaks, their snow-laden ridges stretching into the storm-darkened sky. Competitors from across the world stood at the starting point, hearts hammering in anticipation of the daunting journey ahead. This was no ordinary contest; it was a unremitting trial of endurance, skill and sheer willpower. Rock climbing, high-lining across a gaping void, skiing down near-invisible trails and scaling a frozen waterfall—each phase demanded its own mastery. And all of it had to be done with a heavy pack of essential gear, skis included, strapped to their backs like a second burden of survival.

Abeer's pulse thrummed with excitement, his breath misting in the icy air. He lived for this. The thrill, the competition, the unforgiving wild. Rohil, standing beside him exuded the same electric energy, his sharp gaze locked on the route ahead. The final battle between them had begun.

This becomes even more crucial as Abeer leads the competition with two points, while Rohil trails behind with one. The grand marathon climb is worth two points, meaning whoever wins between them will be the champion of the Frozen Himalayan Competition

The race kicked off with a vertical rock climb. Snow clung to the cliffs, turning every ledge into a slick, treacherous surface. Competitors scrambled up, their fingers and toes fighting for grip. Abeer and Rohil moved with precision their bodies in sync with the unforgiving terrain.

Despite exhaustion weighing him down, Rohil was the first to reach the summit of the rock.

The moment he pulled himself over the edge, the full horror of what lay ahead unfolded before him. A slack rope stretched across a chasm, linking the rocky peak to the snow-covered mountain beyond. The clouds had thickened swallowing everything in a dense blinding fog. The high-line crossing would be a leap of faith into nothingness.

One by one, climbers switched their gear, steeling themselves for the next move. Rohil remained in the lead but doubt flickered in some of the competitors' eyes. A few, overwhelmed by the enormity of the challenge raised red flags, surrendering their place in the race and were rescued by the security choppers.

Then came the wind. Furious and wild, it sent the slack rope into erratic, unpredictable waves. Rohil stepped forward but as he neared the end of the crossing, a violent gust froze him in place. He waited his heart pounding for the right moment to move. The others were catching up fast. Abeer, gripping his rope tightly, had almost caught up with Rohil, challenging his lead. But then the turbulent wind struck him too, forcing him into a statuesque stillness as he fought to maintain his balance in the raging storm. No one dared to move.

Rohil made a snap decision. He shifted his balance, carefully inching his safety hook forward, dragging it from behind to in front of him. It was a dangerous maneuver requiring complete control over his weight distribution. His breath came in sharp bursts as he slowly worked his way forward, pushing the hook ahead and leaping for the rock at the far end.

His fingers slipped.

For a heart-stopping moment he tumbled downward, scraping against the ice. Then—by sheer instinct—his hand found a hole in the rock and he latched on with desperate strength. A stunned silence followed, the other competitors watching in disbelief.

After witnessing Rohil's misstep, Abeer carefully assessed his chances. With precise calculation, he mirrored Rohil's technique but executed it flawlessly, making it across successfully.

Rohil in lead was the first to set foot on the snow-covered mountain.

The brutal chill and the merciless terrain had begun taking their toll on the players. Their bodies rebelled against the insistent cold, the first signs of hypothermia creeping in. Their minds clouded and muscles stiffened. Even Abeer and Rohil were not spared but they had no choice other then to push forward.

The storm soon unleashed its full fury. Winds screamed at nearly 100 km/h, reducing visibility to near-zero. Rohil strapped on his skis, launching himself into the perilous descent. The route was treacherous—littered with trees that materialized out of nowhere through the thick fog. Some racers misjudged their route, colliding fiercely with hidden obstacles. Rohil barely made it through, his body battered by the ordeal. Yet he reached the base of the slope holding his lead over the others.

Abeer followed close behind.

The final obstacle still loomed ahead—the **Frozen Waterfall**. Unlike solid ice this was treacherous, formed by water frozen mid-flow, fragile and deceptive. The concluding ascent was the last obstacle before victory, leading to a daring descent toward base camp. The first climber to reach the finish line would unfurl their country's flag to declare himself the winner.

Abeer and Rohil now shoulder to shoulder launched into their ascent. Ice axes struck against the frozen wall, crampons dug into the brittle snow, carabiners clicked into place with practiced precision. Every movement had to be deliberate—one wrong step and they'd plummet. The storm roared around them but they kept going, defying the limits of their own endurance.

Midway through the climb, Abeer surged past Rohil who was grappling with the treacherous terrain. Battling the fierce wind and snow Abeer made a bold decisive move. For the first time since the start of the Marathon Climb race he pulled ahead of Rohil and the others, seizing the lead and emerging as the frontrunner for the coveted Frozen Himalayan title. On reaching the summit, Abeer's hands trembled as he fixed his skis for the final descent. His breaths came in short gasps—his body was nearing its breaking point.

And then, disaster struck.

Disoriented and drained, Abeer made a critical mistake—striking a loose patch of ice while skiing, triggering a massive avalanche. In an instant, the snow beneath him collapsed and he was swept away tumbling violently, his body battered by the raging white tide. His screams were swallowed by the howling wind as he was buried beneath the heavy snow. Only a fragment of his jacket remained visible. Trapped, his bones aching with unbearable pain, Abeer clawed at the suffocating weight above him, trying desperately to break free.

Rohil, though suffering from his own injuries, pressed on. Every step felt like a battle against his failing body. Before starting his final descent he carefully assessed the loose ice and chose to walk instead of skiing. As he moved forward he caught sight of Abeer struggling beneath the snow, his body barely shifting. Their eyes met. Helplessness flickered in Abeer's gaze. Rohil hesitated, torn between the burning desire to win and the undeniable pull of something greater. The sound of approaching competitors snapped him out of his thoughts. With fierce determination he turned back, surprising Abeer as he hoisted him onto his shoulders.

The descent was brutal. Every movement drained Rohil's last reserves of strength but he refused to stop. Just as the base camp loomed into sight Rohil's body finally gave in. With one last excruciating effort he released Abeer from his shoulders, collapsing onto the snow utterly motionless. Abeer tumbled down the final stretch, rolling uncontrollably toward the finish point. Abeer, barely able to move clawed his way forward on his elbows. The finish line was within reach, but so were the other competitors.

Neet and the others screamed for Abeer to unfurl the flag. Abeer turned back to look at Rohil who lay motionless in the snow, as if silently seeking his approval to claim victory. In that moment it wasn't just about winning—it was about gratitude, an unspoken acknowledgment of Rohil's sacrifice. With exhaustion etched across his face but a reassuring smile still lingering, Rohil mustered the strength to gesture forward, urging him to seize the title.

Abeer glanced back at the oncoming competitors, the race still unfinished. With every ounce of willpower left in him, he forced himself up, ignoring the searing pain in his limbs. He lunged forward grasping the flagpole rope with trembling hands and pulled the rope.

A massive tricolor flag unfurled, confetti bursting into the storm-ridden air. Victory had been claimed—not just for Abeer, not just for the competition but for something far greater. The unbreakable spirit of those who refuse to give up.

The air inside the makeshift hospital at the base camp smelled of antiseptic and melting snow. Abeer sat in a wheelchair, bandages tight around his wounds, his body aching from the Frozen Himalayan competition. Yet, the pain that lingered in his chest had nothing to do with his injuries. For years, he had seen Rohil as nothing more than a rival, a competitor to outpace, a shadow that always ran beside him. But today that rivalry felt different.

Neet pushed his wheelchair forward, guiding him past rows of injured climbers their murmured conversations filling the air. In Abeer's lap rested a trophy—white gold, glistening in the dim light. He wasn't sure if the weight he felt came from the metal or the emotions pressing against his ribs. As they reached Rohil, who sat on the edge of a cot getting his wounds treated, Abeer extended the trophy toward him.

"Even though the title of number one is stamped on me," Abeer said, voice softer than usual, *"I know the real winner is you."*

Rohil glanced at the trophy but didn't take it. Instead, a smirk tugged at the corner of his lips. *"You deserve it, not because you won but because you live for this. Climbing isn't just a passion for you—it's your existence."*

"But you love climbing too," Abeer countered, searching Rohil's face for something unspoken.

"I do," Rohil admitted, *"but it's not my life. My journey is about something else… fulfilling an old promise which I made to my dad."* His eyes flickered to the trophy. *"Besides, I don't accept second-hand things."* He chuckled, though there was no malice in it. "And don't think I did you a favor by letting you win," Rohil said, his voice steady. *"You always wanted a level playing field—you gave me your best trainer,*

shared your years of experience and wisdom." He took a deep breath, a flicker of his old arrogance softened by something new. Then, with a hint of a smirk, he added, *"Well, I leveled it all in a single move. And now, with this victory of yours, we're even."*

Abeer smiles heartly on this and then mutter under his breath, *"Old habits die hard."*

Rohil always liked to have the upper hand in a conversation and he never missed the chance to end it on his terms—*"What you see is what you get."*

Abeer was no different. Though he and Rohil were poles apart in their outlook on life, their foundation was built on the same philosophy—do what you love and excel at it.

Letting out a low laugh, Abeer shook his head. *"Even here, you managed to beat me to the punch."* He took a breath, letting the moment settle before adding, *"If not as a friend, I will always remember you as my greatest rival."*

Rohil met his gaze, something unreadable passing between them. *"I don't think our paths will ever cross again. I'll take you as an experience and move on."*

With that Rohil turned walking away with Mysha. Abeer watched him go, his heart feeling strangely lighter. Neet's arms wrapped around his shoulders, a silent reassurance.

CHERISHED RIVALS

Years passed and the echoes of old battles faded. New memories replaced the old, like fresh snow covering footprints. Abeer and Rohil had moved on carving separate paths.

In the heart of a bustling city, Rohil stepped out of a luxury car, the morning sun glinting off the sleek surface. He entered a towering glass building, the hum of ambition surrounding him. The elevator carried him up and when the doors opened, he stepped into a vast empty office floor—he was the first to arrive. The sign at the reception gleamed under the overhead lights: **'The Adventure App'.** He had built something new, something of his own.

Far away, on a snow-covered peak, Abeer stood at the edge of a cliff. The wind howling against his frame. He was an amputee now, one leg lost to the Frozen Himalyan Competition but he had never stopped climbing. Alongside Neet, he had turned his passion into something greater, running a mountaineering Institute. Teaching others to conquer not just mountains, but themselves.

That evening, he sat by a bonfire with his students, laughter mixing with the sound of a guitar. Flames flickered casting shadows across his face as he stared into the distance. His thoughts wandered, his voice lost in the wind.

"Life is beautiful. Whatever comes your way, accept it. Guilt and worry are wasted emotions—one ties you to the past, the other to a future you cannot control. The best way to live is in the present, surrounded by those who walk with you. Some will stay for a long time,

others will drift away. And then, there are people like Rohil—not like you, but forever a part of you."

As the city skyline darkened, Rohil stood on the terrace of his office, a glass of drink in hand. Below him, the world moved on—cars flashing by. The buzz of his company's first anniversary celebration filled the background. He watched the sunset, the golden hues melting into the skyline, his thoughts quieter than they had ever been.

"I have always worked hard, but Abeer taught me how to truly channel it. Today, I am successful but without him I might have remained just another restless competitor. A wise opponent is far better than a foolish friend."

On the mountaintop, Abeer closed his eyes feeling the warmth of the setting sun on his face. Across the miles, standing on his terrace, Rohil raised his glass, as if offering a silent salute to Abeer. And for a brief moment as Abeer pulled off his face gear and let the cold air kiss his skin, it almost felt as if he acknowledged Rohil's gesture.

In the grand weave of fate, liking and disliking are but fleeting currents, shaping the tides of human connection. It is easy to call someone a friend, just as easy to cast them as a rival. But Abeer and Rohil were neither. They weren't friends, yet they understood each other in ways no friend ever could. They weren't enemies, yet they pushed each other harder than any rival. They were not even strangers, for their paths had crossed too many times, their lives too deeply entangled. They were never meant to stand side by side. But without one, the other might never have risen. And perhaps, in the end, that was the truest bond of all.

THE END